PATHFINDER PERIL

ROCKY MOUNTAIN SAINT BOOK 6

B.N. RUNDELL

**WOLFPACK
PUBLISHING**
— EST 2013 —

Pathfinder Peril
(Rocky Mountain Saint Book 6)
B.N. Rundell

Paperback Edition
© Copyright 2018 B.N. Rundell

Wolfpack Publishing
6032 Wheat Penny Avenue
Las Vegas, NV 89122

Paperback ISBN: 978-1-64119-393-1
eBook ISBN: 978-1-64119-392-4

Library of Congress Control Number: 2018956443

AUTHOR'S NOTE

This is a work of historical fiction. As I always do, I thoroughly research my topic or topics before writing, and so I did with Pathfinder Peril. The main event of this novel is the fourth expedition of John C. Fremont, also known as the Pathfinder. This expedition was undertaken after his scandalous court-martial following his third expedition and was an effort to restore his reputation and credibility. Primarily a political and entrepreneurial expedition to find a year-round route from St. Louis to the West Coast, the pressure applied by his father-in-law, and other investors, and his determination to restore his good name seemed to thwart good judgment.

The names of the expedition members, the dates, events, weather, locations, and occurrences are all historically accurate. Although like any time there are more than one or two accounts, there is considerable variance in the recording of these events. I have given a summation of the accounts and stayed true to the consistent documented history. I have also applied author's license and left out some of the more disturbing details. I do not deem to pass judgment nor condemnation on any of the men, as I was not there, but as hindsight and afterthought often do, suppositions could be made at what would have been a better action or judgment made on the part of all the leaders.

It is historical, as I have explained, but it is also fiction. The fiction is, of course, the addition of our protagonist, Tate Saint, and conversations between the characters. I hope you enjoy and even learn as you read Pathfinder Peril.

PATHFINDER PERIL

CHAPTER ONE
SEAN

"Every time I see the two of them playing, I have to shake my head in wonder. How is it that a massive wolf like that can play so gently with our almost four-year-old, rambunctious little boy and never hurt him is a wonder to me!" Maggie Saint, sitting in her newly fashioned rocking chair on the porch of their cabin, was sharing her thoughts with her husband, Tate. They were watching the cavorting of their only son, Sean, playing with their longtime companion, Lobo, a wolf raised by Tate since he was found in the wilderness almost four years ago.

"That's just one of many wonders the good Lord has blessed us with, Maggie." Tate looked at his beautiful redhead, remembering his first impression of this fiery woman from Ireland. She had come looking for her wayward father who ventured into the Rocky Mountains in search of gold, leaving his wife and daughter in the safety of the civilization of Westport, Missouri. But his wife had passed, and his daughter came West in search of her only living relative, her father, Daniel Patrick O'Shaunessy. It was at Bent's Fort, after the recruiting of Tate Saint by Kit Carson, that Tate met

the flamboyant and brash young woman that was determined to overcome any and every obstacle that came
between her and the finding of her father. And overcome
them she did, and in the process the two realized they were
destined to be together and after leaving her father in the
arms of the Ute Indian woman, Little Otter, they began their
life together in their cabin in the Sangre De Cristo
mountains.

Their almost four years together had been wonderful and
memorable years as they established their home. The cabin
had been built by Tate his first year in the mountains, but
they had added another room, wood floors and Tate
surprised Maggie with a four-pane crown glass window that
overlooked the wide clearing below the house. Maggie had
cultivated a fine garden and had begun enlarging it this
spring, and Tate was looking forward to the birth of a colt
from the little pinto mare of Maggie's. But the greatest joy,
and most time-consuming was the raising of their only child,
Sean. The curly auburn locks topped the chubby-cheeked
face that always seemed to be smiling. The tough little guy
took tumbles, scrapes, and bumps in stride and seldom shed
a tear. He was a joy for both his parents, who savored every
moment with the tireless tot.

They watched as Sean caught up to Lobo, tried to wrap
his chubby arms around the scruff of the big wolf's neck and
wrestle him to the ground. Lobo gave in and dropped to his
side, pulling the boy on top of him as Sean giggled and Lobo
licked his face. Tate remembered his own childhood and his
dog, a big cross breed he named Skipper. The dog was his
constant companion and they spent almost every moment
together running through the woods with his Osage friend,
Red Calf. His mother had been a self-taught nurse who died
ministering to the Osage people during a smallpox outbreak.
After Tate and his father moved to the small settlement of

Springfield, his teacher father was killed while sitting in a game of poker with an itinerant gambler. Tate and his father had shared a dream of going to the Rocky Mountains and spending their lives as mountain men. After his father's death and the mistreatment of Tate by some disreputable villagers, the young man set out to follow that dream and came to the mountains to begin his new life.

As he looked at his favorite redhead and watched his son play, Tate thought about his parents and knew if they could see him, they would be proud and happy for him. He lifted his shoulders in a big sigh, and Maggie asked, "Where were you?"

"Whaddya mean, where was I?"

"Well, you had that glassy-eyed stare goin' on, and you looked like you were miles away!" she remarked.

"Oh, I was just rememberin' my own childhood back in Missouri. You know how it is, lookin' at the boy there brings back memories."

"So, what kind of memories were you thinkin' about?" asked the mischievously grinning redhead.

Tate chuckled and answered, "Oh, just my times in the woods with Red Calf and my dog Skipper. You know, kid stuff."

Maggie smiled broadly, leaned back in her chair and set it to rocking with a push of her toes, and said, "My husband, I'm very happy in our home. This is such a beautiful place. Look down there," she pointed to the valley that stretched out below them, "the green growth of summer is showing, there are flowers galore, the fresh sprigs of the pines fill the air with their scent, and the birds are singing! It's wonderful; I couldn't be happier!" She stretched her arms overhead and turned to smile at her husband.

Tate always seemed to melt whenever she showed that bright smile on her freckled face with her green eyes sparkling. He thought she was the prettiest woman God had ever made. His first wife, White Fawn of the Arapaho, had been pretty, but in a different way. It was shortly after her death that Tate was summoned to Bent's Fort by Kit Carson and the new chapter of his life had begun when he accepted the responsibility of helping Margarite O'Shaunessy find her father. And from his first sight of her, he thought she was the prettiest creature under God's blue heaven.

Tate grinned at his wife, "So, now that Sean is big enough to travel with us, would you like to visit some of our neighbors this summer?"

Maggie turned to look at her husband, "Really? We could do that?"

"Of course, we could, why not? So, who would you like to visit?"

"Well, we could go see White Feather of the Comanche, or Two Eagles and Red Bird with the Caputa Ute. Oh, I know! How 'bout we go visit my father and Little Otter with the Yamparika Ute? Could we do that?" she asked excitedly.

Tate put on his most pensive face and with his chin in his hand, "Oh, I don't know, that's a mighty long way. And, we're not even sure if they would be at their summer encampment. We could wander all over those hills lookin' for 'em."

"Oh, come on! You're an experienced man of the mountains; you can find anybody! You found me father, didn't you?" she joshed.

"Well, maybe, but we'll have to wait a little longer til the days get warmer and more o' the snow's gone. That'll give you time to get the garden cultivated and weeded 'fore we leave. An' you can't be ridin' your little mare til after she foals, an' the colt'll need to get his travelin' legs under him. But maybe after then, we could give it a try." He smiled coyly at his happy wife.

Maggie set the rocker going with her excitement and

began humming the old Irish tune, *Mo Ghile Mear (My Gallant Darling)* a lament for Bonnie Prince Charlie. Tate did not know the words, but he enjoyed the tune as hummed by his sweetheart. She stopped her rocking, looked to her husband, "I'll go fix our supper while you and your son go fetch the horses back. How's that sound?" She was speaking as she rose from her chair and started for the door. Tate's eyes followed her and grinned as he nodded his head.

He stood as she went through the door, "Alright, we'll be back shortly." He reached around the door and grabbed his .54 caliber percussion Hawken and his possibles bag and powder horn. As he slipped the bag and horn over his head, he called out to Sean, "Hey son! How 'bout you and Lobo comin' with me to go fetch the horses?"

The boy jumped to his feet and started his toddling gait toward his father, grinning ear to ear. Lobo was hot on his heels and passed the youngster as they came to Tate. As he motioned the wolf to scout the trail, Tate reached down and grabbed his son's up-stretched arms and swung the boy up to rest him on his shoulders. As Sean grabbed two handfuls of hair, he said, "Let's get Shady!" Shady, the blue/grey Grulla gelding was Tate's horse and Sean's favorite.

The horses were taken to an upper pasture just above the cabin to graze during the day but were occasionally left for a couple of days. This was the first time since spring the horses had been to the pasture and Tate had allowed them a couple of days of grazing on the new growth of grass. Tomorrow they would be hobbled and allowed to graze on the grass near the stream at the foot of the hill. They were almost completely shed of their winter coats, and the long winter had been hard on them. It would take a week or two before they regained some of their winter losses.

As he neared the brush barriers that marked the upper pasture, Tate could hear the horses trotting back and forth.

Something was wrong, they were nervous, but Lobo showed no alarm. He pushed aside the brush to step into the clearing, holding his rifle ready, thumb on the hammer, as he searched for the cause of the horses' concern. He watched the animals, noted one was missing; the little pinto of Maggie's, the one that was in foal. He motioned for Lobo to scout the pasture and started walking the perimeter, searching the trees for any danger.

The wolf stopped, assuming his attack stance with head down, ears forward, teeth bared and prepared to pounce. Tate walked up behind him, spoke softly, "What is it boy, whaddya see?" In the shadows lay the little pinto mare, unmoving. Tate motioned to Lobo, and the wolf slowly stepped forward, watching warily. Tate followed. As they drew closer, it was evident the horse had been slaughtered, probably sometime in the night by a silent killer. After a thorough reconnoiter, Tate came closer to the carcass, saw the teeth and claw marks that told a mountain lion, or cougar, had caught the horse by the throat and quickly brought it down, probably before the horse could even whinny an alarm. Then the big cat had disemboweled the horse, taken the unborn foal, and fled. The carcass lay in a drying puddle of blood. Sean said, "What did it, Daddy? What killed the pinto?"

"A mountain lion, Sean, a big cougar. You know, a great big cat!"

"Ohh," answered Sean, taking a tighter grip on the long locks of his father.

With another quick look around, Tate called Lobo back and started the rest of the horses from the pasture. He would keep them in the corrals near the house this night, but tomorrow, he would have to hunt this cat down. They couldn't have a horse killing cat around, they couldn't lose any more animals.

CHAPTER TWO
HUNT

"Mama, mama, a mount'n lion kilt yer pinto!" declared Sean as he ran into the cabin. Maggie whirled around from her counter with a rag in her hands as she bent down to pick up her excited boy. "I seed it! It was real bloody, too! Yuk!" Maggie stared at her boy, aghast, as Tate stepped through the door. She looked at her man with fear in her eyes as he somberly nodded his head.

"Sorry, babe. Musta happened in the night. All the horses were spooked and stayin' away from the mess," explained Tate.

"I loved that little mare. She was the best horse I ever had," she said as she lowered Sean to the floor.

Tate, with his brow furrowed, looked at his wife, "She's the only horse you ever had!"

"That makes her the best, doesn't it?" she answered as she used the rag in her hand to dab at her eyes. "Well, come on, we better eat, cuz if I know you, you'll soon be huntin' that horse killer."

As Tate slid his chair to the table, his mind took him back to another encounter with a mountain lion, not far from this cabin. He had been felling trees and snaking them back along the mountainside trail when a cougar landed on the back of the horse with the travois. After being kicked free from the horse, the cat leaped at Tate who was armed with only the longbow and it proved ineffective in the close quarters fight with the long-clawed cougar. It took some doing, but he finally prevailed using only his long-bladed Bowie. He didn't want to do that again.

Maggie saw his contemplative expression and asked, "What is it?"

He looked up at his redhead, grinned, and answered, "Oh, just rememberin' the last time I had a set-to with a cougar."

"Oh, you mean the one that left all those scars on your shoulder and side?"

"Yeah, that's the one. But all I had then was my longbow and Bowie. I'm not makin' that mistake again," he resolved as he watched his wife and son seat themselves.

"When ya' goin' Pa? Can I come too?" asked Sean, hopefully.

Tate reached over and tousled the curly hair of his son, "Uh, no, I think you need to stay here an' protect your Ma. Think you can do that?"

"Sure Pa, I can do that. But'cha gotta get me a rifle like yours!" declared the boy.

"Soon, boy, soon. Let's pray now and eat 'fore we starve!" encouraged Tate as he reached for the hand of his son and the other for his wife's hand. With joined hands, they bowed their heads and Tate said a simple prayer of thanks, added a thought for protection on the hunt, and with an Amen, they began their dinner.

After dinner, Tate stepped out on the porch lifting his Hawken to his shoulder, and fired into the treetops. He wanted a fresh load in the rifle and returned into the cabin to tend to it. He cleaned the rifle, then his Paterson Colt pistol and reloaded both. With his pistol on his left hip, his steel-bladed hawk on his right, his Bowie sheathed at his back, and his powder horn and possibles bag crisscrossed over his chest, he stood with Hawken in hand, grinning at his wife.

"You're going tonite?" she asked, somewhat incredulously.

"Yup, he'll probably return to the kill in the middle of the night an' that'll be the best time to get him. It's better'n havin' to try to find him up in those rocks in broad daylight. There's still enough light left, an' with the longer days of summer the moon's gonna be purty big tonite, so, I can find me a good spot and just wait for 'im to show up," explained Tate, with one arm around Maggie's waist as she looked up at her man.

"Well, you make sure you don't get yourself any more scars tonight, understand?" replied the woman as she slapped her man on his back.

"You just get to thinkin' 'bout what you're gonna make outta his hide, cuz that'll be a mighty fine pelt," instructed Tate as he bent to kiss his wife.

DUSK WAS PULLING the last of the light over the western horizon as Tate pushed through the brush into the pasture. He marked the location of the carcass by the trees and worked his way toward the mark. With the bunch grass and random buck brush in the pasture, Tate had decided to take his cover in the open of the pasture, giving him a clear field of fire to the carcass lying in the grass and away from the tree line. The cougar would have to come from the trees to get to the carcass, exposing himself to Tate's sight. But Tate would be hidden behind the brush and downwind of the carcass. Cougars had few natural enemies, and all of them were bigger than a mountain lion. The big cat wouldn't be expecting one from the little cover of the pasture, at least, that's what Tate was counting on as he secreted himself behind the scrub brush.

He was seated, knees drawn up to use as his support for his rifle shot, Lobo lying beside him, head resting between his paws. The Hawken rested across Tate's hips as he scanned his surroundings. With his vision now accustomed to the darkness, the starlight and the rising moon made it easy for him to search the area for any movement. He knew he wouldn't hear the stealthy animal approach and only movement would give the cougar away. It was going to be a long night; the cool of the evening settled into the pasture and wrapped itself around the motionless man.

Occasionally lifting his eyes to the stars to make out the constellations, he was reminded of the nights his father would search the heavens, point out the constellations and make Tate name them. He spotted Ursa Minor, or Little Bear, also called the Wagon of Heaven. The tip of the handle of the Little Dipper, or tail of the bear, or tongue of the wagon revealed the North Star, the star that had been his constant companion all the while during his solitary trip to the mountains from Missouri. But his favorite was Orion, the mighty hunter with his upraised sword ready to slay the lion before him. Tate sighed, lowered his eyes and scanned the tree line, searching for the horse killer.

The night stretched on, and Tate looked to the moon to judge the time. He calculated it to be just after midnight. Now was the time when the cougar should return to its kill, the night was still, even the night birds were silent, and the cicadas had ceased their racket. The low breeze whispered through the pine needles, but in the distance the lonesome call of a coyote lifted in the darkness, making Lobo raise his head to listen. Tate stretched out one leg, then the other, then his arms, trying to move slowly and inconspicuously, but needing to revitalize the circulation in the cold limbs. The stench of the carcass drifted toward him as he reached down and stroked the neck of Lobo, both finding reassurance in the presence of the other.

Tate crossed his arms and rested them on his knees. Growing tired, he lifted one hand to rest his chin on, and relaxed just a bit, just for a moment. Moving only his eyes, he searched the area before him, and his eyelids grew heavy.

It was Lobo pushing against his knee that woke the drowsy hunter. When his chin dropped from his hand, and the jerk of his head startled him awake, he looked first at Lobo, who was in his attack stance with a low rumbling growl coming from deep in his chest. Tate looked to the carcass and saw the light-colored coat of the cougar outlined against the shadowy pines as the big cat sunk his teeth into the haunch downed horse. Tate slowly lifted the Hawken to his shoulder, cocking the hammer to set the triggers, but the click in the stillness of the night caught the attention of the lion who froze to look for the disturbance. Tate stopped his movement until the cat, hearing nothing else, returned to his rotting feast. Tate brought the front blade sight between the buckhorns of the rear sight, centered them just behind the front leg of the cat and touched the front trigger. With a deep breath, letting a little out, he slowly squeezed down on the thin trigger.

Suddenly, flame stabbed the darkness, and the blast of the Hawken shattered the stillness of the night. The rifle belched a plume of grey smoke into the black, and the cougar let out a single cry before it tumbled beyond the carcass. Lobo stood trembling at his side, waiting for Tate to set him loose on the cougar, but the man touched his back to signal him to stay. Tate stood and began reloading the rifle, warily watching for movement in the dark shadows of the pines. Once the rifle was ready, he started toward the quarry, Lobo striding alongside. Tate cocked the hammer to set the rear trigger and slowly approached, knowing the cat could just be wounded and waiting.

Lobo moved away from the man to approach the carcass from the side. Tate came near the corpse of the pinto, saw the sprawled form of the cat just beyond and started to step around the horse when he was struck from behind. Knocked to his face, the rifle discharged as Tate tried to roll to his side, confused. From the corner of his eye, he saw a grey blur as the big wolf launched himself at the attacker. The scream into the night told Tate there was another cougar that Lobo knocked from his back. Tate rolled to get away as the wolf turned to face the cat as it scrambled to its feet. With teeth bared and lips curling the cat crouched, yeowling its cry into the night as the two animals began circling. Lobo moved as the predator he was, his teeth also bared, and eyes cut to slits as he watched the cougar spew its threats. Almost matched for size, the two nocturnal hunters feinted and threatened, looking for an advantage.

Tate scrambled for his rifle and frantically started to reload, more by feel than sight, not taking his eyes from the combatants. He poured powder, patched the ball and seated it, tapped the butt on the ground and with the wiping stick set the ball. He dropped the wiping stick, but before he could pick a cap from his possibles bag, the cat lunged for Lobo. The cougar was crafty and took advantage of the big wolf's off step, with claws extended he launched himself at this intruder to his domain. Lobo was barreled over, and the cat had his teeth in the scruff of the wolf's neck and was digging with his hind feet to get his claws into the bowels of the wolf. Tate drew his Paterson and cut down on the cat, discharging shot after shot into the pale-yellow fur, trying to force the cat to release Lobo.

The cat turned to the new threat in a flash and with a snarl, leaped toward Tate who fired again, point-blank with his Paterson, but the cougar's weight carried it into the man, knocking him on his back and causing him to lose his grip on the Colt. Both man and cat tumbled in a heap, each trying to gain their feet. Tate felt for his tomahawk and pulled it from his belt. The cat had turned and was ready to pounce when the wolf came from the side in a battering-ram charge and sent the cat rolling, as the wolf sailed past. Tate turned and with one lunging step, brought the hawk down atop the skull of the cat, burying it in the animal's brain, killing it instantly. Lobo came back and grabbed at the cat's throat, wanting to ensure the cougar was dead. Tate called the wolf off and dropped to his knees to hug the big Lobo.

When he regained his strength, Tate slowly stood and went to fetch his Hawken. He placed a cap on the nipple, lowered the hammer and sat the rifle against a nearby tree. Slipping his Bowie from the sheath, he began the skinning process of the first cat.

Shafts of daylight were bending through the trees behind the cabin when Tate and Lobo walked into the clearing. Maggie was rocking in her chair when she saw her man, and she quickly stepped off the porch, running to the pair of hunters that were bearing the rolled-up hides of two cougars. She stopped before Tate, saw the red and with hands on her hips said, "That better not be your blood mister!"

"Well, I don't think so, but you might have to check me out to be sure!" he declared with a mischievous smile.

CHAPTER THREE
PLAYMATE

TATE WAS AWAKENED BY SOME NOISE COMING FROM THE clearing in front of the house. He was not alarmed, knowing Lobo would have alerted him of any danger, but something was happening, and his curiosity was aroused. He rolled from under the blankets not wanting to disturb the slumbering Maggie and with only his union suit and socks on, tiptoed to the front door. He snatched up his Hawken, leaning against the side wall, and slowly opened the door to the pale morning light. Lobo ran by the steps, turned, and dropped down with his chin between his front feet, and his rump in the air, as he watched the clearing. Tate stepped out on the porch to see Lobo jump up and take off running around the edge of the clearing with a ball of fur chasing after. *What is that?*

As his eyes became accustomed to the dim light, he watched two playmates running and chasing around the clearing. The appearance of a cinnamon bear cub startled Tate, and he searched the tree line for any sign of the cub's mother. The way the two were acting, they appeared to be lifelong friends. First, the cub would chase Lobo, then the wolf would take after the cub. Each one would playfully nip at the other's haunches as if they were playing tag and then the antics continued. Within moments, both were tired and crumpled in a heap, side by side, breathing heavily. Lobo noticed Tate sitting on the porch and rose from his rest and trotted to the porch, easily mounting the three steps to drop beside Tate, now seated in the rocker. The bear cub sat up, watching his friend, then decided to join them on the porch. Tate stayed in his chair and with one hand resting on the head of Lobo, watched the bear cub come onto the porch and drop down beside the wolf. The cub leaned back against Lobo, and fell over on the wolf, as Lobo accepted the nearness of his new friend.

Tate looked the bear over, judging he was between two and three months old, maybe recently weaned, but looked very healthy. His thick fur was a brownish red hue with the tips of the fur fading to almost tan. He was a cinnamon bear, one of the black bear family, but unique in his coloring. But this age was too young to be independent, his mother had to be somewhere nearby, and with the cub on the porch, things could get a little dangerous. Tate again searched the tree line for any sign of the mother bear but saw none.

With his Hawken in his lap, Tate continued to stroke the head and neck of Lobo as he rocked back and forth, thinking. His eyes were on the clearing when he felt something cold and wet on his hand and he turned to see the cub sniffing his hand and touching it with his wet nose.

"Uh, be careful there buster, that ain't your breakfast," declared Tate softly, not wanting to startle the bear. But the cub pulled back and looked up at Tate, cocked his head to the side and examined this new creature in his world. Tate guessed the cub to be close to sixty or seventy pounds, and big enough for more than just his mother's milk. But he wondered whether to feed the furball or not, if he's orphaned, he would need sustenance but, if not, Tate didn't want him to become accustomed to getting food at their house. He motioned to Lobo to stay, and he slowly rose from the chair and walked back into the house.

He was stirring around the counters when Maggie came up behind him and asked, "Whatcha lookin' for?"

"Oh, just something to feed the bear cub on our porch."

"Oh, well, there's some left-over stew and some corn-bread," replied a sleepy-eyed redhead. Then she looked up at Tate with her brow furrowed and asked, "What'd you say?"

"I was lookin' for somethin' to feed the bear cub on our porch," he drawled, seriously.

"Sean's still in bed! He's not on the porch," exclaimed Maggie.

"Not that bear cub, the cinnamon bear cub with Lobo," said Tate, nodding his head in the direction of the porch as he filled a tin plate with some stew and cornbread.

"You've got to be kidding me! There's a bear cub on our porch?" asked a now wide-awake Maggie.

"Yup, come see for yourself. Only, stay behind the door and watch," directed Tate as he started for the porch. Maggie padded behind him, pulling her housecoat close around her and pushing the hair from her eyes. Tate stepped through the door and she held the it as she watched. Tate slid the pan beside the outstretched paw of Lobo and the stubby foot of the bear, stepped back and sat down in the rocker. As the curious cub looked and sniffed at the food, he would glance up at Tate, back at the food, and satisfied it was for him; he began to dig into the feast. It was evident the cub was hungry, and Lobo just watched his friend consume the it without interfering. When he finished, he sat back on his haunches and appeared to rub his tummy in contentment as he looked up at Tate and licked his lips to say thank you.

"Oh, look, he's happy!" said Maggie from behind the door. The cub turned his head and looked over his shoulder at the door to see the woman grinning at him. Maybe it was the red hair, or the tone of voice, or the wispy housecoat, but the cub was instantly interested in this newcomer and rolled to his feet and started to the door.

"Don't let him in!" instructed Tate, firmly. "Either shut the door, or come outside, but don't let him in the cabin."

Maggie stepped through the door and went to her knees holding out her arms as the bear approached. He went straight to her and began licking her face as a delighted Maggie began giggling and stroking his fur.

"Looks like love at first sight," declared Tate. "But be careful, those are sharp teeth and long claws, and we don't know where his momma is and if she shows up she'll be one jealous momma bear!"

Maggie had pulled the front door shut as she came onto the porch, but now it opened, and Sean stood, rubbing his eyes as he stated, "I'm hungry!"

He hadn't seen his mother with the cub, but she turned and said, "O.K., I'll come fix you something to eat," and stood to face her son. The boy just turned away, and Maggie followed him back into the cabin, pulling the door shut behind her. She giggled a little as she steered the hungry waif to the table to be seated to await his morning feeding.

"So, are you awake now?" asked Maggie as she watched Sean finish his cornbread muffin and chokecherry jelly.

"Ummhumm, I'm am," replied the boy.

"Well, I've got something to show you, it seems Lobo has found himself a playmate!"

"Playmate?" asked Sean, as his mother put his moccasins on and slipped his buckskin shirt over his head.

"Ummmhummm, a playmate. Come'on, I'll show you, but we have to be very quiet."

Maggie led the boy, his hand in hers, to the door and slowly opened it to see the porch. Tate turned as they did and motioned for them to come out. As they stepped onto the planks, Maggie saw Lobo and the cub playing in the clearing and Tate watching with a wide grin across his face. Maggie lifted Sean to his father's lap, and Tate turned the boy to see the new friends chasing one another. Sean stared, smiled and looked at his mom and back at his dad and said, "That's a bear!"

"Ummmhummm," answered Tate. "Sure 'nuff. It's a cinnamon bear, but we don't know where his momma is, so we have to be very careful."

"So, what do you think about his momma?" asked Maggie, as she watched the two tireless playmates.

"I dunno, she might have been hurt or even killed, or she might be a new mom and not know what to do. Maybe she abandoned him, or maybe she's lookin' for him. We'll just have to wait an' see. We can't be gettin' too attached or too friendly until we know more."

"How long do you think that'll be?" asked Maggie, knowing her son would want to try to play with the cub.

"Oh, we'll probably know in three or four days. If she doesn't come lookin' for him, it'll be because she can't."

"Do we feed him in the meantime?"

"Yeah, I think he might be weaned, but he's not big enough to find his own food yet."

"Don't they eat just about everything?" inquired Maggie.

"Purty much. Berries, bugs, grubs, stuff like that," explained Tate.

"Now where am I gonna get those things? It's too early for berries, and I'm not going after bugs an' grubs!"

"Well, maybe me'n Sean can look for them, but Buster'll eat anything else you wanna feed 'im."

"Buster? So, you've already named him?" asked the redhead.

"Gotta call 'im somethin' now don't we?" asked a grinning Tate, winking at his boy.

"IT'S BEEN TWO DAYS AND STILL NO MOMMA!" EXCLAIMED
Maggie as she watched the bear cub and Lobo playing in the
clearing. The family was sitting on the porch steps, Maggie
and Tate sipping their evening coffee, and watching the pair
romp. "I just can't believe she would abandon her cub."

"Maybe she didn't have a choice, maybe she was hurt or
even killed. It's not unusual for a momma bear to die
defending her cubs. I once saw a boar grizz attack a cub, and
the momma lit into him like a tornado, but not before he
killed one of her cubs. Course after it was all over, he wished
he hadn't, but the damage was done. Now, if that cub's
momma was younger, she mighta had a couple cubs an' a
boar attack her an', well, you know. . . " explained Tate.

"I just wish there was something we could do, maybe try
to find her or something," declared a frustrated Maggie.

"Well, I was thinkin', mebbe we could take a little trip.
With him taggin' along, could be the momma'd get his scent
and come get him. We'd have to be careful, but it
might work."

"Really? Oh, that would be great. And even if we didn't

find her, at least I'd know we tried," answered the redhead. "Where will we go?"

Tate chuckled, "Ya know those hot springs I told ya' 'bout?"

"Aye, you told me but never took me there."

"Mebbe we oughta give it a try. That'd take us all along the face of the Sangres, an' if we take our time, we could make it there an' back in 'bout three days."

"When? When do we go?" pleaded Maggie, excitedly.

"How 'bout first thing in the mornin'?" answered Tate, chuckling and grinning at his anxious wife.

Maggie leaned against her mischievous husband, laying her head on his shoulder. She reached over and pulled Sean close against her, and the three watched the playful duo in the clearing.

SEAN SAT in front of Tate, chubby legs dangling on each side of the pommel, as they made their way through the trees on the narrow game trail that skirted the shoulders of the Sangres. Maggie followed close behind on the rangy bay that had served as their packhorse as they followed the scout of Lobo. Buster, the bear cub, would lumber after Lobo, then sit down on his rump to rest while Tate and Maggie caught up, then off he would go again in pursuit of the easy loping Lobo. The cub seemed to want the assurance that the rest of his adopted family was still following, and he hadn't been abandoned. Once he saw them coming, then away he would go.

The trail they followed was just inside the tree-line on the lower skirts of the mountains. The Sangre De Cristo mountain range, with its granite crags that seemed to scratch the blue sky, still held considerable snow above timberline and the white of the glaciers stood out against the cobalt blue canopy. It was a beautiful and cloudless day. The aspen were in full display with their pale green leaves, held on the tips of the white skeletal branches, and clusters of quakies colored the deep blue timber sided mountains with splashes of green. The crisp air of the mountains carried the fresh scents of pine, aspen, and the muted aromas of elk and the bitter stench of bear.

Lobo returned from his scout and sat beside Buster at the side of the trail. When Tate spotted the two, their contrasting images were stark against the buck brush behind them. Lobo with his lean rangy, even sharp features that were distinctly different from the rounded and sculpted figure of the cub. While Buster, seated on his rump and holding his forepaws against his chest, stood about four feet tall, Lobo, in the usual pose of a wolf at ease on his haunches, was head and shoulders above the cub. But they had become the best of friends and were always within a quick call of one another.

"We'll camp over yonder," said Tate over his shoulder pointing to the grove of aspen with a grassy clearing next to the small stream. "We're close to the hot springs, so we've got lotsa time. Mebbe we can find some bugs and grubs for Buster."

Maggie made a face at the thought of bugs and answered, "Maybe you can find some, not me! I'll look for berries and such."

The horses were picketed within reach of the fresh grass, packs stacked, and bedrolls laid out before the group started for the stream below the tree line. Sean was holding tight to his mother's hand, and Tate had his Hawken resting on his shoulder as he motioned for Lobo to scout ahead, with Buster following close behind. As they neared the edge of the trees, Tate spotted a downed tree that was starting to rot, and he called Lobo and Buster back. The two watched the man as he used his Bowie to break-through the grey wood to the soft decay beneath. He motioned for Buster to come closer, but the cub just looked at him. When Lobo came near, the cub followed, and Tate pointed to some grubs in the crumbling rust-colored wood. The cub was instantly interested, and caught the first one in his teeth, then began digging with his claws in the soft mass, finding more tasty treasures. When it appeared Buster had exhausted the supply of his treats, he sat back and looked to Tate for more, only to be disappointed. It was not in him to search for his own tidbits, the lazy nature of the beast showed in his expectant look as he waited for direction from his replacement momma.

The grassy slope draped from the timber to the willows at creekside where the meandering stream slowly carved its way south. Tate lifted Sean to the ground, picketed the horses, and sat beside Sean on the grassy knoll. They watched as the cub shuffled behind Maggie as she led the way to the water. She knelt at the edge of the bank and started picking some early summer strawberries, handing them off to the hungry cub. Lobo sat back, cocking his head from side to side as he watched the feeding of the cub, occasionally licking his lips expecting his share.

Tate handed Maggie his Hawken, "Hold this, I'll see if I can get us some fresh trout for supper." He got down on all fours and crawled to the edge of a cut-back bank where the stream made a wide bend around a sandbar. He lay on his stomach, bellied closer to the stream and slowly reached down into the water. His arm was just long enough to go a little over elbow deep as he cupped his hand back toward the bank. Going strictly by feel, he gradually moved his hand under the cut-back. He felt the smooth underside of a nice trout, slowly slid his hand forward and as he neared the gills, he snatched his hand up, grasped the meaty trout and brought him topside, throwing the fish onto the grass. The cub quickly went to the trout, still flopping in the tall grass, and caught the fish with his teeth and sat back to tear away the scaly skin and begin his feast.

Tate had watched the cub take his catch, then turned back to Maggie and said, "I'll throw the next one in your direction, see if you can keep it away from that hungry furball."

Within a short while, Maggie was protecting eight nice trout from the two four-footed playmates. Although Lobo had shown no interest in the fish, Buster tried to steal another but failing, he lumbered off with his friend. Maggie cleaned the fish as Tate stood and stretched, looking over their surroundings. Tate suddenly crouched, reaching for the Hawken, as he cautioned, "Be quiet and still. Sean, come over here to your mother." On the other side of the willows, Lobo and Buster had stopped their play and stood still, staring at a big boar grizzly standing erect and looking at these intruders to his territory.

The big bear, standing over eight feet tall, held his forepaws before him as he cocked his head to the side and let out a roar that seemed to shake the nearby pines. Three grunts followed his threatening roar as Buster ran back into the willows toward Tate and Maggie. Lobo dropped into his attack stance, head forward and low, teeth bared and lip curling back, eyes cut to slits and one paw lifted as he stared back at the beast of the mountains. Another roar from the bear declared his prominence, and he dropped to all fours and slowly sauntered up the grassy slope and into the trees. Lobo and Tate both relaxed and looked to one another when the wolf came through the willows to rejoin his family. Buster was lying beside Maggie as she ran her fingers through his thick fur on his neck. The cub had apparently dismissed the threat of the grizzly and was enjoying the protective caresses of the redhead.

With their attention on the grizzly, Tate was startled

when a voice from across the stream said, "I see your family has grown!"

Tate whirled around, dropping into a crouch and bringing his rifle to the ready; when he recognized the familiar figure of his friend and relaxed. "Two Eagles! Good to see you my friend, and Red Bird, this is a surprise."

Maggie jumped up and waved Red Bird to come over, which she gladly did, pushing her appaloosa mare into the shallow water. When the two came from the stream, Red Bird quickly dropped to the ground and found herself in the warm embrace of her friend, "Morning Sky, it is so good to see my friend. And how is the wife of Longbow?" Tate and Two Eagles clasped forearms and greeted one another. Maggie said, "Oh, you must come to our camp and visit. We've got some fresh trout and some smoked buffalo, please come!" pleaded Maggie.

Red Bird put her arm around the redhead's shoulders and answered, "We will, we will. We have much to talk about; it has been a long time."

Maggie smiled broadly and nodded her head as she went to fetch the trout and start for the camp.

Maggie and Red Bird led the way as Tate with Sean on his shoulders, and Two Eagles led the horses and followed. Maggie had noticed a difference in Red Bird and asked, "Uh, are you...?"

Red Bird smiled and nodded, rubbing her slightly protruding tummy. "Yes, finally!"

Maggie giggled at her friend and said, "I'm happy for you Red Bird. You're going to make a great mother. So, tell me everything that's happened since last we talked!" The two women's incessant chatter provided the undertone of the welcoming visit as Tate and Two Eagles watched the women and spoke intermittently with one another.

"So, were you two headed to the same place as we were?" asked Tate.

"If you mean the hot springs, then yes we were. When we saw you coming from the trees, we saw Morning Sky's hair and knew we had to come see you. But we did not think to see that big grizzly you ran off. And what are you doing with a bear cub?"

"Oh, he just came into our clearing and was playing with Lobo there. No momma, just him. And the two seem to be best friends. We thought maybe this little ride would flush out his momma if she was anywhere near, but no luck. Could be that old grizz done her in," explained Tate.

"First you have a wolf, and now a bear, what's next?" chided Two Eagles, laughing.

Tate chuckled as he answered, "Hopefully nothing. But ya' never know. I wouldn't be surprised if the boy here," motioning to Sean, "brings home one of everything he finds."

"You need a good name for the little one. One that tells who he is," stated Two Eagles.

"Isn't it the custom of your people for the brother of the father to choose the name?" asked Tate. Two Eagles looked at his friend as he realized what he was asking.

CHAPTER FIVE
FRIENDS

MAGGIE AND RED BIRD, BUSY AT THE WORK OF TANNING THE cougar hides, were chattering away as if they had known each other for many years. The hides had been coated with the brain solution and the women were stretching them across the edge of the shale slabs at the end of the clearing. As Maggie listened to Red Bird tell of the people in her village and the antics of the children as they played the hoop game, she remembered the first time she met Red Bird. She and Tate had been hunting in the valley and came upon Two Eagles and Red Bird as they tended to their kill of an elk. When Tate and Two Eagles greeted one another as friends, Tate introduced Maggie. Red Bird had been staring at this white woman's flaming hair and she was surprised that Maggie spoke in the native Ute language. When the redhead explained their friendship with the Yamparika Ute and that the chief of the village, Lame Buffalo, had conducted the joining ceremony for Maggie and Tate, Red Bird allayed her suspicions and curiosity, eagerly becoming friends with Maggie, or Morning Sky as she was known among the Utes.

The two had grown to become close friends and often visited one another.

"My man said if our boy was as clumsy as that one, he would tell the others he was not the father!" Red Bird was laughing, as she thought of the boy in her story, who had tripped over the hoop. Her laughter brought Maggie from her reverie, and she joined in the mirth with her friend.

"Don't worry, once your son is here, that man will do nothing but strut and brag about what a great warrior and hunter his son will become," explained Maggie. "Tate is that way with Sean already, even though the boy can barely walk, he's already wanting to take him hunting. And Sean's just as bad, it was all I could do to keep him from going with his father when he went after these cougars!"

"When will my sister have more little feet running after that wolf?" asked Red Bird with a coy smile showing. She had not missed a draw of the hide across the rock edge as she talked, but was busily watching the hide stretch and the hair move on the golden pelt of the cougar as she waited for an answer to the question always asked by women of one another.

"Oh, I don't know, maybe soon. I've been using that tea made with the puccoon plant, and it has worked very well, so I'm certain I'll not be with child any time soon. We just want time to be with Sean before we have another," answered Maggie.

ACROSS THE CLEARING, Tate and Two Eagles were fashioning new arrows from the alder branches cut on their way back to the cabin. Tate had crafted some arrowheads from metal retrieved from a burnt wagon they found when coming from the Bayou Salado back to the cabin and handed them to Two Eagles for his approval. When he used the blade of the point as a knife on the calloused heel of his palm, he lifted his eyes to his friend, "These are good. They will serve you well when you go after your elk in the fall."

Two Eagles had prepared a small fire and fashioned a cone of hide stretched over some willows to capture the smoke and heat. He took each shaft, held it over the smoke and moving it back and forth, used his critical eye to shape and straighten each shaft. Then he rolled the shaft on a flat rock, to cool it and complete the task. After smoking the shafts to straighten them, he would hold each shaft up to the sun, twirl it to ensure its straightness, and nod and grunt his approval. Once the shafts were complete, he handed each one to Tate. Using his razor-sharp Bowie, he would split the end of the shaft for the point, insert it and wrap with a thin strip of rawhide to secure it. Then he would start applying the fletching and the arrows would be complete. The men worked well together, and seldom spoke, always intent on their work.

Two Eagles looked across the clearing where the women were working and asked Tate, "Why do women talk so much? We work just as long and say little. They talk all the time!" he nodded his head in their direction to emphasize his point, then shook it in wonder.

"Oh, they talk about babies, men, and everything in between. But I know this, don't try to figger 'em out, cuz men have been tryin' to do that forever, and we'll never know much more'n we already know, which ain't much."

A distant sound caught the attention of both men as they froze to listen. There it was again, the sound of hooves clattering on stone; someone was on the trail below the cabin. Their home sat on a timber covered shoulder of the tall mountains that shadowed the broad expanse of sand dunes. Behind the dunes, the mountains dipped into a cut that held a well-used game trail that led over the Sangre De Cristo's and into the wide grassy valley beyond. Although the trail was well-hidden and unknown by most, it was one of four crossings of the mountains and could be found by an experienced mountain man or Indians. Sometimes it was used by the Arapaho to come into the San Luis Valley to hunt buffalo or as a route for raiding parties.

Tate and Two Eagles quickly stood, motioning to the women to be quiet and corral Sean. They grabbed their weapons, Tate his Hawken and Two Eagles his bow. At Tate's command, Lobo stayed with the women as they retreated to the cabin, Sean in tow.

The men trotted through the timber silently, each step muffled by the fallen pine needles. Once in sight of the trail, they dropped to one knee and peered through the timber, looking beneath the low branches of the ponderosa and fir to see the movement of several horses. They moved alongside the trail, searching for enough of an opening to see the riders. Within moments, they stood behind tall ponderosa and watched as the horses came into view of the break in the trees. A bearded white man, attired in buckskins, and looking like a man of the mountains, rode the lead horse, but the others were heavy-laden packhorses, four of them.

Tate called out, "Hold up there!"

His shouted command startled the rider who immediately reined up his horse, causing the packhorses to bunch up behind him, as he twisted in his saddle searching for the challenger. Tate stepped from behind the tree, rifle held at the ready and began walking toward the stranger. The rider lifted his free hand, holding to the lead rope of his pack train and the reins of his horse in the other.

"Don't mean no harm, I'm just a trader up from Buzzard's Roost, down at Hardscrabble. I was plannin' on meetin' up with some o' the Utes an' doin' a little tradin'. Didn't know there was any white man in the country. Muh name's Alexander Barclay, most call me Lex."

"You ever traded with 'em before?" asked Tate as he drew closer, looking over the packs and the stranger.

"No sir, never have. But I'm hopeful. How 'boutchu? Needin' anything? I got just 'bout anything ya' need," he stated as he waved his hand toward the heavy loaded mules.

While the two were talking, Two Eagles stepped from the trees and stood before the man on the trail. When the trader turned around and saw him, he was startled and bounced in his saddle, "Scared me!" He looked to Tate and asked, "You two together?"

"Yup, I'm Tate Saint, and this is Two Eagles of the Caputa Ute."

"Saint? Are you the one they call the Rocky Mountain Saint?" asked the trader.

"I've been called that," answered Tate. "If you're wantin' to trade, follow this trail," he pointed downslope, "and you'll find a trail that cuts back just past some buckbrush. Follow that back up thataway, and you'll come to my cabin. We'll meetchu there." He turned away, and he and Two Eagles quickly disappeared into the trees, leaving the trader staring into the woods. The two men loped through the woods and came to the cabin's clearing, laughing at the expression of the trader. Tate called to the women, "Company comin'! Ya' might wanna come out and see what he's got!"

The door opened, and Maggie walked to the rail of the porch and asked, "Whadaya mean, see what he's got?"

"He's a trader and says he's got anything you might want," explained Tate, grinning. Maggie looked back at Red Bird smiling and motioned for her to come out. The women laughed as they came down the steps with Sean and Lobo and Buster following. This would be the first time a trader had come to them. Usually, any trading required a long journey to places like Bent's Fort and the thought of trading here at their own cabin was exciting.

"Well, well, this is mighty fine! I never expected to see such a fine place up here in these mountains," exclaimed Barclay as he rode into the clearing. "Yessir, mighty fine," he added as he started to step down. But with a quick thought, he looked at Tate and asked, "Is it alright if I get down?"

Tate nodded, and the man swung his leg over the horse's rump and stepped to the ground. Tate looked at the women and said, "This is my wife, Maggie, and our friend, Red Bird, Two Eagles' wife."

Barclay doffed his floppy hat to reveal a bald dome and nodded as he said, "Pleased to meet you ladies. Now, what might I interest you in? I've got just about everything you may need!"

CHAPTER SIX
TRAVEL

THE TRADER BARCLAY'S VISIT WAS A DISAPPOINTMENT TO TATE and Maggie. He had loaded his packs with trade goods more suitable for the Indians, not knowing of any whites in the area nor of Tate and family. The Saints had little need for vermillion, beads, pots, blankets, and other geegaws and doodads that were popular with the Indians. His supply of flour, beans, sugar, and lead, the staples desired by Tate and family, was a small part of his load and insufficient for their needs. But the trader agreed to follow Two Eagles and Red Bird back to their village and trade with the Ute, which was what he wanted anyway.

As they waved goodbye to their friends, Tate turned to Maggie and said, "I guess this means we'll be making that trip to Bent's Fort after all."

"Yes, but what are we going to do with Buster? We can't take him with us, can we?" asked Maggie.

"Why not? He's gettin' bigger an' can move along as fast as a walkin' horse. We won't be in any hurry anyhoo. 'Sides, I don't think Lobo'd let us leave him behind, even if we could."

"How soon do you want to go?"

"Oh, I dunno, nothin' keepin' us here, guess we could leave just anytime, I reckon."

Maggie dropped her head and chuckled as she spoke, "The last time we went, Sean was just a babe in the cradle-board. This will be quite a trip for the little guy."

Tate twisted in his chair to look at his redhead, "Uh, you mean Little Bear?" remembering the name given by Two Eagles, "The mighty little one that runs with wolves and bears?" looking at the trio of playmates romping in the grass.

Maggie smiled as she watched the three inseparable friends. *Sean may not have a lot of children around to be his friends, but he has something even more rare and special with those two,* she thought. "Well, if we're goin', I guess we better start gettin' ready!" she declared as she started back to the cabin.

IT WOULD BE at least a two-week trip for the strange entourage. Tate had decided to take a slightly different route and go over the nearby pass from the sand dunes that would take them over the Sangres, instead of taking the more traveled wagon road that had become known as the Sangre De Cristo pass. All the while he was readying the animals, his mind repeatedly traveled to the other trips made to Bent's Fort. Remembering his first journey West and his stop at the fort that had been fortuitous in his meeting Kit Carson who would become his friend and mentor, made him hope they would meet again. It was Kit's insistence that he take Maggie on the hunt for her father that brought him together with his lovely redhead, and the thought of it brought a smile to his face.

"Now, what has you grinning?" asked a curious Maggie as she carried an armload of their supplies to the corral fence for Tate to pack.

"Oh, just rememberin' the first time I saw you at Bent's Fort."

"And just what is it that made you smile?" she asked, her voice sounding like the music of carillons in the early morning.

"When I first saw you, my first thought was, 'that woman's trouble!'"

"Well that certainly turned out to be prophetic didn't it?" she declared as she took the stance of hands on hips and fire in her eyes but a slight smile to her lips. "Boy, howdy, it did!"

She reached down and grabbed a horse apple and chucked it at him, causing him to hunch his shoulders and duck.

"See what I mean?" he chuckled. "Always into mischief!"

Sean had been just a few steps behind his mother, also holding an armload, but his little legs didn't carry him as fast as hers, and as he approached the corral and saw his Mother throw the horse apple, he said, "Ma! You said not to play with those!"

Maggie whirled around laughing and answered, "You're right, Little Bear, you're right. I won't do it again." She took the bedroll from her son and lay it beside the other gear that awaited the packing. She turned to see her little boy, standing tall and proud with his thumbs under his galluses, and watching his father pack. "So, what's got you so puffed up?" asked Maggie as she grinned at the boy.

"Huh?" answered Sean, puzzled by her question.

"Well, the way you're standin' there, you look mighty happy or proud about something, what is it?"

"I like my Indian name, Little Bear!"

Maggie smiled and bent to take her son's cheeks in the palms of her hands and pulled him toward her as she kissed him full on the face. The boy grinned but pushed her aside, so he could watch his daddy. Maggie paused a moment to look at her man and her son, thinking how happy and blessed she was with her fine family.

The sun was full up when they finally got underway, Sean sitting in front of his mother, crowding the two of them in the saddle seat, but she was happy with his nearness. The boy was full of questions, asking about everything he saw that was new to his young eyes. The call of a bird, the color of a new flower, the shape of a rock formation, the scamper of a small animal, all of them piqued his interest and brought forth a barrage of questions.

Tate was leading the pack string of two horses, one a big piebald black and white mare, the other a bald-faced sorrel. Maggie and Sean were aboard the bay and Tate on his mousy colored Grulla, Shady. Tate thought they were making good time, better than he anticipated with Buster ambling along behind Lobo. The first two days brought them out of the mountains, and the prairie stretched out before them. It was getting late on their third day of travel, and he decided it was almost time to find a camp. He reined up to take a good look at the area before them.

"Look Mama!" shouted Sean as he pointed to the flats. "What are them?" he asked as he watched the herd of tan and white animals, many lifting their heads at his question.

"Those are antelope, or some call them pronghorns," answered a smiling Maggie, appreciating her son's insatiable appetite for knowledge.

"Do bears eat annewope?" asked the boy.

"I suppose they could, but I don't know if they could catch one. They're very fast."

Sean looked down at Lobo and Buster, both lying on their bellies for a short rest. "Wudju Buster? Wudju eat a annewope?" Getting no reaction from his friend, Sean squirmed around to look at his mother and declared, "Nope, we don't eat annewope!"

Maggie hugged her son, smiling at his childish ways and talk, but proud of him anyway. She looked to Tate to see if he had listened to the conversation, only to see him grinning at her and his son. She hugged him again only to cause him to squeal, "Momma, that's 'nuff!"

Tate motioned to the riverbed to the right of their trail, indicating it would be the location of their camp for the night, and kneed his horse forward and Maggie followed. Although Lobo had learned to share with his friend, his efforts at catching a few jackrabbits provided little enough for the two and Tate knew he would have to do a little hunt as soon as they made camp. He had seen plenty of the prong-horns and also knew the river bottom of the Cucharas would probably be a good place to get a deer.

After stripping the horses of gear, Tate took his longbow and quiver of arrows to begin his hunt, always conscious of the need to be as inconspicuous as possible. They were in contested territory: with the Kiowa to the southeast, Comanche directly south, Arapaho north and who knows what in their immediate vicinity. He chuckled to himself as he walked from their camp, leaving Lobo and Buster with Maggie as she readied a cookfire and got the coffee going. He didn't think this hunt would take very long; it was the time of day for the deer to head to the water for their evening drink. He muttered a simple prayer as he walked downstream along the river's edge, holding close to the willows and moving silently.

Maggie had gathered a couple of armloads of dry cotton-wood branches and Sean copied his mother with his load of smaller sticks. Lobo stayed at their side, but Buster was tuck-ered out and had opted to stay with the horses and take a snooze. Maggie dropped her armload at the fire and heard a growl come from Lobo. She looked at the wolf and turned to see what he was growling at and spotted a ragged looking coyote stalking their camp.

She was only two steps from her Hawken and quickly picked it up, cocking the hammer as she lifted it to her shoulder. Lobo dropped to his attack stance and took a couple of steps forward to threaten the much smaller coyote, but the ragged dog-like creature kept coming. The scrawny beast was wide-eyed, his fangs were bared when Maggie saw the animal had a crazed look in his squinty eyes and he was leaving a trail of slobbers from his foaming mouth. She instantly recognized the coyote was rabid and even more dangerous. Lobo started to move, "No Lobo! Stay!" she commanded. The wolf stopped, but never took his eyes from the coyote. Maggie lowered the muzzle to take aim, took a quick breath, and squeezed off her shot. The rifle bucked and snorted a cloud of smoke. The explosion filled the clearing and startled every bird within hearing causing them to take wing. She dropped the butt of the rifle to the ground to immediately start reloading, even before the smoke cleared. Moving simply by memory and feel, she poured the powder from the measure into the muzzle, grabbed a patch and ball from the possibles bag resting on her hip, seated the ball and grabbed the ramrod just as the smoke cleared enough to see the rabid coyote was down and unmoving. She rammed the ball home, quickly replaced the ramrod and snatched a cap from the bag, seated it and looked again at the coyote.

Lobo was itching to get to the animal, but Maggie grabbed a handful of fur to hold him back. It was all she could do to keep him from wresting free and charge the coyote. She knew he would sink his teeth into the carcass to ensure it was dead and would easily contract the rabies carried by the mad animal. Maggie dropped to one knee beside the wolf and calmly spoke into his ear to settle him down. When the wolf finally looked at her, she got him to sit down and become quiet and still. She rubbed his neck and patted his chest, encouraging him to focus on the attention he was getting instead of the coyote.

Tate came running into the camp, holding his bow before him, arrow nocked, and swiveled his head searching for the cause of the blast. Maggie pointed, "He's rabid! Be careful!"

Tate walked to the carcass, poked it with his foot, and was satisfied the coyote was dead.

"You did good! Just keep Lobo there while I get rid of this."

CHAPTER SEVEN
TRADING

FOUR MORE DAYS OF TRAVEL BROUGHT TATE AND FAMILY TO Bent's Fort. After crossing the Arkansas River well upstream of the confluence with the Purgatoire, they rode along the upland toward the massive adobe structure of the trading post that dwarfed the many lodges of the different bands of Indians that surrounded the fortress on the plains. It was a familiar sight to both Maggie and Tate with the only change being the number of Indian camps.

They stopped on the crest of a slight rise that gave them a panoramic view of the area and Tate pointed out the different camps, identifying them by the type of lodge and the markings on those lodges. "On the north there, the largest camp is of the Arapaho, and those to the west of them are probably the Cheyenne. The camp to the east, I'm thinkin' that's Kiowa, and the large camp south of them's the Comanche. This is the only time an' place you'll find that many different tribes together and not wantin' to slit each other's throat!" explained Tate.

"There's so many! Last time we were here, there were just a few, but now, I never dreamed there would be such numbers!" declared Maggie as she looked over the awesome sight.

With hundreds of cookfires, each with a spiraling thread of smoke twisting into the blue with no breeze to stir them, Maggie thought the scene was of one suspended from the heavens by hundreds of threads, like an unraveling bolt of cloth.

Tate looked over the bluff to the river below, and seeing a broad swath of grassy bank amidst a cluster of cottonwood and willows, he motioned as he spoke, "How 'bout we make camp down there an' keep those two mischief makers," pointing to Lobo and Buster, "away from the others. I don't think too many folks would like to see a bear come strolling into the fort."

"Yeah, I can just imagine what a ruckus that would cause," replied Maggie.

It was a pleasant camp, back from the river and shaded by the rising bluff to the north. The tall cottonwoods provided both firewood and shade, and the marsh to the east had cattails aplenty. Maggie looked forward to using the new shoots and roots of several to complement her planned supper. She also spotted some Indian potato and was already making her plans to harvest several to add to the meal. After the long winter, it was a joy to be able to make a meal with something more than smoked buffalo meat or even fresh venison. She did find a couple handfuls of strawberries and hoped to find more as Sean loved them.

After picketing the horses, Tate brought several armloads of firewood to the fire ring fashioned by Maggie and worked with his flint and steel get the tinder and kindling started. Maggie watched, smiling as her son stretched out on his belly beside his father as they both blew on the sparks in the tinder to get the fire going. With his chin resting on his palms, elbows in the dirt and his feet moving back and forth as they pointed to the sky, she thought her son was an exact duplicate of his father. Both had dark brown hair to their shoulders, gentle eyes, and a ready smile that made instant friends. She was proud of her men and thought she would like to have a dozen more just like them, but that was a thought that was best postponed for now.

The sun set on the western horizon and turned the sky to brilliant shades of orange and gold. Maggie stood mesmerized by the colors and watched as the river was turned to liquid gold when the colors arched overhead. She had always been filled with the wonders of the Creator when He took the time to say goodnight with such splendid displays of His majesty. Tate came to her side, slipped his arm around her and pulled her close to enjoy the display together. She leaned her head on his shoulder and spoke, "The sunsets here are so beautiful, the colors are so, so, brilliant! God seems to enjoy painting the end of the day."

"I believe you're right about that! It's almost like He's sayin', 'There, another great day done!'"

Maggie smiled at his remark, enjoying the closeness of her husband, and looked down at Sean as he held to the pant leg of his father and declared, "I like orange!" pointing to the horizon.

Maggie bent and picked up her son, setting him on her hip and said, "Then you get to come help your momma fix our supper!" She walked back to the fire ring to fetch the coffee pot, and hand it to Tate, "You get the water, I'll start the rest."

The family and their menagerie enjoyed the repast of meat and vegetables with everyone getting their fair share and fill. After the clean-up work was done, they sat by the fire absorbing the warmth as the chill of the early summer evening tried to penetrate their clothes while they talked of the duties of the coming days. Maggie knew she would stay in camp with the animals and Sean but hoped she would have some visitors. She asked Tate to promise to tell any of their friends that were nearby to come see her as she was feeling lonesome for womanly companionship. Understanding her need, he smiled at her confession and readily agreed.

As TATE STARTED to step down from the saddle, he was greeted by a familiar voice, "Well, if it ain't Tate Saint! Glad to see you my friend!" Tate instantly recognized the voice of William Bent as he stepped from the shadows of the catwalk over the walkway. He extended his hand as Tate freed his foot from the stirrup and turned his direction.

"Howdy, Mr. Bent!" he replied.

But before he could say more, Bent said, "William, or Bill, but not that Mr. Bent stuff. How many times I gotta tell you?" chided the man, grinning at his younger friend. "Come down for some supplies, have you?" he observed, looking at the empty pack saddles on the horses.

"Yessir, sure 'nuff. Had a trader from Buzzard's Roost stop by but he didn't have what we needed, so here we are," answered Tate. "How's the family?"

"Reckon you haven't heard, but Owl Woman's crossed over. Little more'n a month, now. But her sisters, Yellow Woman and Island are still with me. Island's doin' a fine job with the kids, but we all miss Owl Woman," explained Bent.

"Mighty sorry to hear that. It's not an easy thing to bear, losing a wife," empathized Tate.

"That's right, you lost your first wife didn't you. So, I guess you do understand."

"Yessir, sure do," nodded Tate.

Bent looked around and asked, "Didju bring that redheaded spitfire with you?"

Tate chuckled at the description, "Yup, she's at our camp yonder by the river. She made me promise to tell anyone we knew to come see her. Ya think Yellow Woman and Island would like to go?"

"I'm sure they would, but I don't understand. Why didn't she come here to the fort with you?"

"We didn't think a big wolf and a yearling bear would be too welcome," grinned Tate.

"A bear? You had the wolf, but now you've got a pet bear?" asked Bent, incredulously.

"Yeah, he kinda adopted us, an' try as we might, couldn't find his momma and the boy has made a pet outta him, so we couldn't leave him behind, and, well, you know how it is with kids."

"That I do, yessir, that I do," declared Bent, shaking his head and grinning. "Wal, you go 'head on an' get your supplies an' I'll tell the wimmen folk they got comp'ny. They'll probably wanna go see her right away." He waved his hand as he turned to go to his quarters. He stopped and turned back around, "Say, after you're done in there, come on up to the game room. I got somebody I'd like you to meet." Tate nodded his head and waved as he stepped under the catwalk and into the trader's store.

Once his supplies were loaded, Tate walked to the far corner of the compound and climbed the steps to the game room in the second story quarters. Bent stood as he entered and motioned him back to the corner table with two other men, both older than Bent. As Tate approached, "Tate, I want you to meet two of the orneriest old mountain men that ever walked these hills. This long tall drink o' water is William 'Old Bill' Williams." The tall, lean man stood and towered a full head over Bent as he extended his hand to shake with Tate. "And this other'n is Uncle Dick Wooten!" Wooten stood and shook Tate's hand as well. After all were seated, Bent said, "This young man is the one Kit Carson talks about as the Rocky Mountain Saint!"

"I've heard such talk, but sometimes ya gotta be careful whatchu believe when it comes from that little runt!" said Old Bill, referring to Kit. "But at least he says good things 'boutchu."

"And I've heard considerable talk about the two of you. Accordin' to what I've been told, you were a minister of the gospel and spent some time with the Osage. That right?" asked Tate as he looked to Old Bill.

"That's true."

"I have some good friends with the Osage. Jeremiah Tallchief and his son, Red Calf. Red Calf and I practically grew up together," explained Tate.

"Wal, it shore is a small world, ain't it? I know both Jeremiah and Red Calf. I spent some time with them. I married A Ci'n Ga, and we had two daughters. My name with the Osage was Lone Elk. Course, all that was probably 'fore your time, cuz when I knew Red Calf, he was only 'bout so high," he explained as he held his hand at about three feet from the floor.

"Yeah, when I saw Red Calf last he was 'most as tall as you!"

The men spent most of an hour getting acquainted, but Tate had to bid his goodbyes and leave. With full packs, the horses trailed after Tate as he led them from the fort. Instead of heading directly back to his camp, he pointed Shady toward the Comanche encampment. He was greeted by two young warriors that stopped him before he could enter. Tate leaned his forearms on his saddle horn and looked at the two, asking them in their own language, "Who is it that stops Longbow from seeing his friends?"

Both of the men were startled, and as their faces showed both surprise and relief, the older one said, "I am Fat Porcupine, and this is Lazy Otter. Who is it that you want to see, Longbow?"

"Is your shaman White Feather?" he asked.

Porcupine nodded his head and said, "She is our shaman. Her tipi is next to that of Raven, our chief," pointing to the central compound of the village.

"Raven is your chief? Is the man that was your chief before Raven not with you?" asked Tate, respectfully refraining from using the name of one that had died.

"He has crossed over. Raven is now chief," answered the young warrior somberly.

"Then I will see both your chief and your shaman. Go, tell them Longbow comes!" he instructed. The two young warriors quickly turned and ran to the lodge of the chief to carry the message.

"Longbow, my friend. It is good to see you. It has been too long since we talked. Come, sit, and we will talk," declared Raven, the chief of the Comanche village, as he motioned to the blankets and willow backrests. "My woman will make us some food."

"So, my friend Raven is now the chief, and he has taken him a woman. I am glad for you, my friend," replied Tate as he followed the chief to the backrests. Tate first met Raven when he helped the Comanche during a smallpox epidemic in Tate's first year in the mountains.

As he started to seat himself, another voice caught his attention, and he turned as White Feather, the village shaman, spoke, "So, Longbow has come," as she approached with a wide smile and arms held out to greet her friend. "It has been too long. You and Morning Sky do not leave your cabin to see friends, that is not good." It was a mischievous smile that painted her face as she stepped back from hugging Tate. "And what has brought you to our camp? And where is your woman?"

"All in good time, woman. You ask too many questions of

our friend," chastised Raven, speaking to his sister. White Feather slapped her brother on his shoulder as she took a seat nearby; the two had always been close and often sparred with one another. Tate had become like a brother to them, although at one time he could have become the mate for White Feather, but her duty to her people as a shaman came first.

"We did not know you were here, but our trip for supplies has given us the opportunity to be together, and I am thankful," responded Tate as he looked at White Feather. *She is just as beautiful as ever, maybe even more so,* he thought. "But, since the great Comanche are here, and no people have better horses, perhaps I might trade for a couple. I do need a mount for my woman and my son."

"Then they are here! I would see Morning Sky and your son," said White Feather as she looked around for his family.

"They are both down at our camp," he motioned toward the river, "and are anxious to see old friends. She would like it if you came to see her."

Feather stood and said, "I will go now." Without any hesitation, she went to her lodge, came out with a small bundle, and left without another look in Tate's direction.

"Let us go look at the horses," said Raven, rising from his seat. He nodded to his woman, already busy at the cookfire, indicating they would soon return. As they walked, the men were quiet. It was not the way of the Indian nor the mountain man to dally in small talk. When so much of their life required stealth and silence, it was the quiet communication and understanding between men that was shared by these two long-time friends. They had been through much together and had proven their worth to one another on hunts, in battle, and in times of loss and trial. Words were not necessary for these men to connect.

The herd was returning from the river, being driven by

the young men, and Tate and Raven looked them over as they passed. As Tate expected, all were fine stock, for the Comanche were known for their horses, the result of many raids to the ranches in the south along the Mexican border, and their own selective breeding. Several fine horses caught Tate's eye, one especially, that he recognized as the big black stallion that was Raven's warhorse. It was an impressive animal with a broad chest, long mane and tail, well-built and standing over 15 hands high. Then two others got his attention. One was a dapple-grey mare of about 15 hands and the other a smaller, maybe 14.3 hands steel-dust. Tate pointed them out, and Raven grinned, "They are both good animals, the mare is from my stallion, and the grey is her colt." He motioned to the young men to cut out the two and bring them over.

As Tate closely examined the horses, he was reminded of a breed from Spain he read about as a young man. That breed was the ancient Andalusian, and these horses had many of the traits including a broad neck, massive chest, short back and strong, broad rump. The dapple had three stocking feet, and the steel-dust was marked and built like his mother. Tate was pleased with both horses and turned to Raven and said, "Let's work on a trade, shall we?" They led the horses back to Raven's lodge, tied them off and sat down to the meal prepared by Raven's woman, Red Blossom.

When the meal was finished, Tate went to his packs, pulled out a blanket wrapped bundle, and returned to the fire. He lay the package at Raven's feet and watched as the chief unwrapped the gift. Tate was pleased to see the reaction of Raven as he lifted the new Hawken rifle to his shoulder and looked up at his friend with a smile. When he flipped back the last fold of the blanket to see a new powder horn, a cloth bag with lead balls, percussion caps, and patches, he carefully lifted them to examine each item. Then his eyes fell on the Bowie knife with scabbard, and he picked it up, pulled it from the sheath and checked the blade's sharpness. He tried to temper his excitement when he looked at Tate and said, "You want to trade this for the horses?"

"No, Raven, that is my gift to my friend."

"Ahhh, it is good. This is a fine gift," replied the chief, nodding his head. Both men knew what the other was thinking and that whenever a gift is given, it is expected that a gift of equal or greater value will be given in return.

As the men did their dealings, Red Blossom busied herself with the clean-up, but when she saw the gift from Tate, she too knew what was expected, and she dropped her head to stifle a giggle, knowing her man was honor-bound to give the horses in return. But that was the way of men, and she thought women were more direct and honest with one another. Yet she respected her man and his friend and knew this game of always trying to outdo one another, would only strengthen their bond of friendship.

Raven looked at the Hawken, then to the tethered horses and back to Tate with uplifted eyebrows. Tate nodded his head, and the two men grinned. Raven stood, and the men clasped forearms to the words of Raven, "It is done!"

"Good, then how 'bout you and Blossom bring those two horses with you when you come to our camp for a meal later?" Raven glanced at a smiling Blossom and back to Tate and nodded his head with an affirmative grunt.

WHEN TATE RODE into their camp, he saw Yellow Woman, Island, and White Feather visiting with Maggie while the three of the four Bent children played with Sean and Lobo and Buster. It was an idyllic scene, and Tate knew Maggie was enjoying the time with other women. Maggie greeted him with a kiss and returned to the visitors as Tate stripped the horses. When he finished, he went to the fire to pour himself a cup of strong java and told Maggie that Raven and Blossom would soon come and would stay for supper. That news prompted the four women to work together to prepare the evening meal.

CHAPTER NINE
WASHINGTON

"As you know, John, my colleagues and I are one hundred percent committed to the expansionist movement. And now that we have the treaty Guadalupe Hidalgo that ended the Mexican war, there are over half a million square miles that need to be opened to settlement," he waved his hand to stop the perceived interruption, "Yes, I know, I know, there have been many settlers that have taken to the Oregon Trail and are even now working to settle the northwest. But we need more! Now, once before you mentioned your dream of having a coast to coast railroad, and that's been mentioned by others. But before we can do that, we need funding and a plan. That's where you come in." The speaker seated himself behind the massive desk in his senatorial office and reached for his humidor and one of his imported cigars. Senator Thomas Hart Benton was the powerful chairman of the Senate Committee on Military Affairs, but his concerns were more than just military. Considering cigars as his only vice, he was used to forcing his will upon others, but had run into some opposition from his son-in-law, John Charles Fremont. The senator tended to his cigar as John rose from his seat and walked to the map on the wall beside the senator's desk.

At the age of 34, Fremont had already made a name for himself as an explorer and adventurer. The map on the wall was one of seven produced from his explorations and findings and published by the Senate a year earlier. Most considered Fremont a handsome man and now as he stood before the senator, he was dressed in long striped charcoal trousers, topped by a waistcoat of dark charcoal over a starched white shirt with a maroon and grey ascot. His black double-breasted frock coat hung to mid-thigh and accented the tailored cut over his tapered frame. With a well-trimmed full beard and wavy dark hair that rested on his collar, Fremont was the picture of fashion. He pointed to the map, placing his finger on St. Louis and dragging it across the map to the west, he said, "The 38th parallel is a direct line from St. Louis to San Francisco. I believe we can find a route that closely follows that line for the first railroad to the west coast!" He stepped back with his left hand on his hip and holding his coat open. His broad smile showed his ever-present confidence that was at once his strong point and greatest weakness. Often thought of as arrogant, his confidence and strong will had enabled him to accomplish more in his young life than men of greater renown had in their entire lives.

"But can it be a year-round route? Aren't the winters bad in the mountains?" asked the senator between puffs that emitted considerable smoke in the confined quarters.

"I believe so, I've been to that area," pointing again at the map in the area marked the Great Basin, "several times and in all seasons, so, yes, I believe so," declared Fremont.

"Now, let me tell you what we're up against. After that nonsense with Kearny and California, some of my colleagues are a little gun-shy about appropriating any money if you're involved," and as Fremont started to interrupt, the senator waved him off again, "and yes, I know President Polk reinstated you, but those things don't just go away. So, this is what I suggest. I will give you a list of names, many of whom you know, for you to contact and see if you can't solicit their financial support, if needed. That way, we won't waste any time. Then, you can proceed with enlisting those you need to go with you. Am I understood?" The senator rose and walked from behind his desk with his hand outstretched. As the men shook hands, the elder statesman added, "And, as always, give my love to my daughter, Jessie."

"Yessir, I will. I will get started with these names right away, and I see some of them are in St. Louis, do you want me to go there to see these gentlemen?" asked John.

"Wouldn't St. Louis be the better place to outfit your expedition?" asked the senator, grinning and showing his own confidence in gaining the funding. The senator was so committed to what was being called "Manifest Destiny," he was certain his other expansionist colleagues would see things his way and ante up the needed appropriations. The need to expand the borders of the United States from coast to coast and to settle all the territory recently gained, was a primary goal for this new nation. Benton and his fellow senators believed they were called by God to see this nation established and settled.

Fremont turned and picked up his silk top hat and with a curt nod, left the senator's office. With his head abuzz with ideas and hopes, Fremont made his way to one of his favorite pubs where he planned to meet some of his friends. The corner pub known as O'Reilly's was a regular meeting place for young adventurers and entrepreneurs of the day, and Fremont was pleased to see the Kern brothers, Richard and Edward, waiting for him. They stood at the bar and lifted a glass as he entered to signal him to come over. Edward was the first to speak, "So, where is the intrepid explorer off to this time?"

Fremont motioned to the barkeep to bring a brew and turned to the brothers, "Another expedition to the mountains. I hope to find a passageway for a railroad to follow the 38th parallel from St. Louis to San Francisco!" he declared as he brought his fist down on the bar, bouncing the empty glasses and making the others grab for their drinks.

"San Francisco! Jolly good! And when do you plan to leave?" asked Richard.

"Well," and John looked pensively down at the bar top thinking, "that depends on when we get the funding. But, if everything goes well, we'll be leaving in two, no more than four, months." He lifted his head smiling as he made his announcement to his friends. "And, I want you two to go with me!"

Richard and Edward looked at one another, and Edward grinned as he answered, "We were hoping you'd say that. What an opportunity to record that great adventure in oils for the world to see! Everyone has been amazed at your reports, but to see it in color with all its splendor and panorama, that would be magnificent indeed!"

The brothers slapped each other on the back and Richard looked to Fremont, "What about Benjamin? Could he come as well?" Fremont knew their older brother Benjamin and knew he was a medical doctor and hard worker and would be an asset on the journey. He was known as a skilled physician, excellent horseman, and a quick learner.

"Yes, I believe he would be a great help on the journey," answered Fremont, grinning.

Although all three men were roughly the same age, anyone that witnessed their displays of excitement and enthusiasm would have thought they were full of youthful enthusiasm. But their excitement was contagious, and when

Fremont offered to buy drinks for the house, the entire pub exploded with gusto.

"So, tell us about the expedition. Where will we go?" asked Edward.

"We'll jump off from St. Louis. We'll take the Sante Fe trail to Bent's Fort in the territories. Then we'll re-supply and head due west. That will take us over the Rockies and the Great Basin and the Sierra Nevadas and into California. If we're lucky, we'll make it by this time next year."

The brothers looked at one another, and although Edward had been on Fremont's third expedition, they were finding it difficult to comprehend a journey that could take most of a year, but the appeal of the adventure outweighed their concerns, and they slowly grinned at one another and slapped hands and said together, "Sounds great!"

"Good! Well, there's much to do so I must be on my way. As you prepare, make sure you have good warm clothing because we will be crossing the mountains in the middle of winter, and that's not going to be easy," he warned. But their excitement could not be dampened, and they nodded their heads as they shook his hand. Fremont marched out of the pub with his top hat sitting at a jaunty angle and swinging his walking stick as if it were a baton. After his embarrassment with the fiasco with General Kearny, which was a dispute over who was to be the military governor over California and resulted in the court-martial of Fremont, later over-turned, he was determined to restore his reputation and going on another expedition was just the answer.

CHAPTER TEN
RETURN

MAGGIE LEANED DOWN AND STROKED THE NECK OF THE dapple-grey mare, sat up and looked over at Tate who was watching her with a wry smile on his face. She smiled back at both her men, Tate held Sean between him and the pommel, and said, "Yes, I like my new horse. She is beautiful, this mane and tail will require some care, but she is so beautiful, and her gait is the smoothest ever!" While Tate led the string of packhorses, she led the steel-dust that would one day become Sean's horse. She looked back at the rangy yearling colt and added, "And that one's a beauty too. I can't wait to see Sean aboard him."

"Well, that's gonna take some doin', but I plan on Little Bear being right beside me as I do a little trainin' and tamin' of that colt. I also think we might use him to help start a herd of our own. Maybe catch some o' them mustangs in the valley, breed 'em with him, could make some good stock for tradin' an' sellin' to some o' them pilgrims."

Sean squirmed in his seat, "Pa, when we gettin' home?"

"Oh, we got a few days yet, Little Bear," answered Tate, grinning at his impatient son.

Traveling across the rolling hills of the sage-covered prairie, they rode side by side and used the opportunity to educate the youngster. Sometimes Tate would point out a plant or animal and quiz the boy about the name, and other times Maggie would ask simple questions like, "What's this?" as she pointed out the parts of the horse, saddle, or other gear. Often making games of the learning, Sean would readily respond and with a correct answer would often puff with pride as his parents praised him.

During a lull in the wilderness education, Maggie said, "Freckles is still a little skittish with Lobo and Buster, but I think she'll get over it soon," as she reached down to stroke the mare's neck.

"Freckles?" asked Tate.

"Yes, Freckles. That's what these spots," pointing to the coloring of the mare, "or dapples as you call them, look like and since both of us have freckles, I thought that would be a good name, don't you?"

"Good as any, I s'pose. What're ya' gonna call the colt?"

"Oh, that's up to Sean. It's going to be his horse, so, he should name it. Right?"

Lobo and Buster were together well out in front of the others when Lobo jumped a big jackrabbit from a thick cluster of sage. When the long-eared rabbit took off at a zig-zag run, Lobo was hot on his trail. The wily pilgrim of the prairie used every dodge, turn, and obstacle to his advantage. The chase switched directions faster than Tate and Maggie could follow as they stood in their stirrups to watch the rabbit take the wolf on a tour of the rugged terrain. The rabbit had turned and was making a twisting and turning attempt at escape that brought the pair back to the waiting group. Almost before they could react, the rabbit ran under Maggie's new mare, between Shady and the pack-horses, and into the sage on the other side of the trail.

The dapple-grey was startled at the rabbit and started to rear up, but when she spotted the wolf coming directly at her, she launched herself into the air, twisting in the middle and kicking out as she grabbed for footing where there was none. Maggie saw the wolf coming and pulled back on the reins, taking a quick dally around the saddle horn and had latched onto the horn with a death-grip with the other hand and took a deep seat, sticking her feet well into the stirrups, prepared for what she knew was going to happen. She wasn't disappointed, but she was scared. When the mare came back down to earth, she tried to tuck her head between her front legs, but the dally with the reins kept her chin against her chest, and she couldn't drop her head. As she started to rear up again, Maggie shifted her weight forward with her face almost in the mane, and she reached down to stroke the mare's neck as she talked calmly in her ear to settle her down. The rabbit and wolf were long gone as the mare twisted and turned, sidestepped and danced around in a tight circle searching for any other thing that might be a danger. With Maggie continuing to stroke her neck and talk to her, she began to settle and with a couple of snorts, stopped her prancing. With another, "Good girl," from her rider, the mare calmed and visibly relaxed.

Tate had been forced to keep a tight hold on the lead ropes of the packhorses and maintain control of Shady, all with a boy in his lap. But the Grulla was used to Lobo and hadn't been startled, although the packhorses were a little flighty, but the taut lead kept them in control. Now as Tate looked at his favorite redhead, he let a grin cross his face and said, "That was good! For a while there I thought you were gonna have to sprout wings to come back to earth!"

Maggie's smile split her face as she beamed from the praise from her husband, "I had a good teacher. And it helped that I saw them coming, so I expected something."

"What you did, keepin' control and all, did more for that horse than any amount of training. Now, she's gonna trust you and depend on you. I think the two of you are gonna be a good pair," observed Tate. Few riders could have handled that kind of explosion with a scared horse, but she did, and he was mighty proud of his wife.

As they talked, Lobo came trotting back with the jackrabbit hanging from his mouth,appearing to grin at his success. He went ahead of riders to join Buster, who had seated himself to patiently wait for his friend to return. The chasing of rabbits was best left to the fleet of foot rather than the roly-poly furball, but he was quite willing to share the feast with his buddy.

The two furry friends were making short work of the mid-afternoon snack as the others rode by their makeshift dinner table. The growling and snarling of the two, no more than siblings arguing over the best tidbits, made the horses eye them as they walked by, but none were spooked enough to shy away. Tate spoke to Sean, "What do you think of that, son?" motioning toward the scrapping pair.

"I wike mine cooked, don'tchu?" answered the boy.

Tate chuckled and answered, "Yup, shore do. Cooked is definitely better." He was glad the boy saw the struggle as nothing more than getting something to eat. Others might be concerned about the rabbit, or the killing, but it all was the way of life in the wilderness. Tate was pleased the boy already understood that simple matter as a part of living. He already knew the boy had a heart for animals, after all, how many youngsters had befriended a bear, and knew under other circumstances the boy could just as easily befriend a rabbit. But to be able to differentiate between the need of killing to eat and caring for God's creatures was something even adults struggled with sometimes.

Their trail followed the Huerfano River, a rather shallow

and twisting river lined with cottonwood, alder, willows, and boxelder. Tate was anxious to get out of the flats and into the trees of the mountains, and his sights had been set on the long ridge that fell from the cone point north of the river bottom. He pointed, "That cone up there is 'bout two, mebbe three miles from the bottom yonder. Where that ridge drops off at the river is where we'll be campin' tonight." He shielded his eyes from the bright summer sun that had dropped to just above the hills and added, "Ol Sol will be settin' soon, and we should be there 'bout dusk."

Sean piped in with, "Good, I'm hungry!"

Maggie chuckled at her son, who seemed to amaze her daily with his rapidly growing vocabulary and many expressions. "And just what do you want for your supper?" she asked.

"Meat 'n tatoes," declared the hungry boy, rubbing his belly.

"O.K. then, I'm sure we can do that just for you," replied Maggie, grinning.

Their campfire was near the riverbank, and while the strips of meat dangled over the low burning fire and the potatoes simmered, Maggie and Sean waded in the shallow creek, digging their toes in the sand and splashing one another as they giggled. Both Lobo and Buster got in on the game, and the four shortly made a muddy mess of the shallow water. Tate watched as he reclined on the grass, leaning on one elbow and laughing at the antics of his family.

Supper was soon over, clean-up finished and everyone in their bedrolls by the time the fading light of dusk dimmed to darkness that slowly revealed the tips of tiny diamonds set in the velvet blackness overhead. Tate took advantage of the clear night to point out some major constellations to Sean, but the stars and Tate's descriptions were lost on the tyke, who soon fell asleep to his daddy's droning voice. When he saw his son's eyes close, Tate looked to Maggie, and they smiled together with pride in the boy.

The rising moon was waxing full as the shadows stretched across the grassy clearing that held three sleeping forms side by side. The horses were picketed between two big cottonwoods no more than fifteen feet away, and Lobo and Buster were stretched near Tate. The nervous horses were stomping, and Lobo rose and growled as Tate reached for his Hawken. He whispered, "Easy boy, what is it?" as he looked in the direction of the wolf's stare. Lobo's head was down, lips curled, and eyes squinted as he stretched himself into a fighting stance. Buster had rolled to his feet and lumbered off toward the trees and the horses. Tate looked into the darkness of the trees and three sets of orange eyes, catching the glowing embers of the fire, stared back. Lobo stretched out a step, growling with each move. Tate came to his feet, cocked the hammer to set the triggers of the Hawken and with a quick glance, assured himself the cap was on the nipple and the rifle ready to fire. He tucked the Paterson in his belt and in a crouch started toward the unmoving eyes. Lobo matched him stride for stride, and Tate caught a glimpse of Buster slowly moving with them, his head down and teeth bared as he stared into the dark. Lobo let loose a loud, threatening growl as a challenge to the intruders.

The eyes had moved apart, watching the man and animals approach. Tate heard an answering growl, no, more than one, come from beyond the edge of moonlight. Suddenly, three wolves stepped into the ring of light, ready to do battle. The lead wolf, a ragged looking black, was the largest of the pack, but still smaller than Lobo. The three stopped, and the black's head slowly moved to take in the three before him. Tate was certain the black was confused at the sight of a man, a wolf, and a bear. Tate held his rifle hip high, pointed at the level of the wolves, moving it back and forth with his finger on the thin trigger where the slightest pressure would cause a discharge blast of lead and smoke.

Suddenly the second and smaller wolf lunged, and Tate's bullet caught it in mid-flight. The explosion seemed to make even the trees flinch, and the smoke followed the lead messenger of death. The wolf crumpled in a heap, causing the other two to balk, but Lobo would not be stopped as he hit the black in a charge that knocked the lead wolf of the pack to the ground, with Lobo's teeth locked on this throat. With a sudden jerk and snarl, the bigger Lobo ripped the throat from the startled black, that spasmed in death. When Lobo attacked, Buster charged, but the last wolf quickly spun, dropped his haunches and with tail tucked, quickly disappeared into the trees. Buster stood on his hind legs, front legs paddling as he burst forth in a growl that echoed through the trees. With a grunt, he dropped to all fours and padded back toward the now wide-awake Maggie and Sean. He dropped down on his belly and stretched out for Maggie to stroke his fur as his reward.

Tate looked around, making sure there were no more threats, and dragged the two carcasses back into the trees and well away from their camp. Lobo joined Buster and when Tate returned, Sean was petting the pair while Maggie was reassuring the horses with her calm voice as she touched each one. Tate looked to the moon, judged the time, and said, "Well, we probably won't get any more sleep tonight. We might as well pack up and see if we can't get a little closer to home. Who knows, we might even get to sleep in our own beds before another day's done."

Maggie hugged her man and her son, one on each side, and said, "That would be wonderful, wouldn't it Sean?"

"Ummmhummm," answered the sleepy-headed little boy as he wrapped his little arms around his momma's leg.

CHAPTER ELEVEN
PREPARATIONS

"THIS IS MY FAVORITE TIME OF YEAR," OBSERVED MAGGIE. SHE and Tate were sitting on the porch, sipping their morning coffee and enjoying the colors of the rising sun. They were facing to the west and the colors they witnessed were those reflecting the pinks and reds of the sunrise at their back. With a colorful swath of gold in the aspens below the cabin and on the slopes to the south blended with the paint of the morning light, she breathed deeply as she watched the brush of the Creator dip into His palette and color the mountainside. Far across the San Luis Valley, the San Juans and their foothills caught the morning glow with their snow-laden peaks and golden aspen covered hillsides and caused Maggie to catch her breath at the beauty. She thought she had never seen such beauty and she marveled at the wonders of God's creation.

"I would have to agree with you on that. It is a beautiful time of year. It's kinda like God is saying, 'Alright, get ready for that long winter rest', as if we all should hibernate like the bears."

"That would suit me!" smiled Maggie. She lifted her steaming cup of coffee as if to toast the truth.

Tate raised his as well, "Yeah, but I'm thinkin' we could use a little more meat in our stores in the cavern yonder. We probly' got 'nuff, but if we have a hard winter, which I'm thinkin' we might, it could also be a long one. So, I'd feel better if we had, oh, mebbe a couple more elk or so."

Sean crawled up on his dad's lap, turned around and plopped down, making his dad grunt at the impact, and asked, "We go huntin'?"

"Mebbe," answered his dad, "it probly wouldn't hurt for us all to go one more time." By all, he meant to include Lobo and Buster, the bear. The cub could no longer be called a cub, even though he still had the personality of one, for he was getting close to four hundred pounds. Tate had wondered what he was going to do about the bear's usual penchant for hibernating, but he figured he would just have to take his cues from the young bruin's behavior.

"Well, if we're goin', we better get with it, cuz I shore don't wanna get caught in an early snowfall. From the looks of the mountains already getting their tops frosted, we'll be gettin' it purty soon!" observed Tate as he looked to his wife. She was sipping her coffee and looked over the cup at him with an expression that told Tate he would just have to wait until she was ready. He grinned at her but relaxed and leaned back in his chair and sipped his own coffee contentedly.

Tate knew the elk would be moving down to the valley floor to escape the high mountains storms, but the bigger herds usually stayed in the upper end of the valley where there was better protection with the close-in timber. He was hopeful they would find a few stragglers closer to home and make it easier to fill their need. With two packhorses in tow, Maggie and Sean doubled up on Freckles, Tate moved slowly on the trail that held just inside the tree line along the skirts of the Sangres. He held his hand up to stop, and everyone, including Lobo, seemed to freeze in their tracks. Tate had watched Lobo, knowing he would pick up the scent first, but Tate had detected them almost simultaneously with the wolf. Then he heard them, several elk coming down a long draw, were crashing through the timber paying little heed to their surroundings. Something had spooked the elk and Tate swung down, rifle in hand, ground tying Shady as he waited for the elk. He motioned for Maggie to join him and she was quickly at his side. He listened as the small herd came through the timber. Their chosen path was taking them through the aspen on the opposite ridge and were easily seen by the hunters but did not afford them a shot. Tate motioned for Lobo to come back, sat Sean down on a large flat rock and told Lobo, "Stay, guard Sean." Lobo obediently dropped to his belly beside the boy and lay his head on Sean's lap as an anchor. Tate nodded at the wolf and turned toward the tree line to see the herd beginning to mill about in the grassy plain, but the herd bull watched the trees for any sign of pursuit from whatever had spooked them.

"Why were they running?" asked Maggie in a whisper.

"Don't know, coulda been a grizzly or some wolves, but whatever it was, I think they left it far behind. You take that point right there," motioning to a bit of an exposed shoulder of rock, "that'll give you a good shooting position, and you won't be far from here," motioning to the boy. "I'm goin' to cross over and down on the other side of 'em. I'll take the first shot with my bow, and I'm hopin' I'll get another shot, either with the bow or my rifle. Either way, they'll probably push back into the trees right under where you'll be an' you'll have a shot." Maggie nodded her understanding and started toward her designated place with a backward look to her son as he waved at his mom.

Just a short while later, Tate was in position and chose a

cow without a calf and a young spike bull as his targets. He stepped into his bow and the arrow whispered to its mark, making the startled bull jump sideways, and stagger a few steps before sinking to his knees and falling, legs splayed. Before the bull had fallen, Tate had another arrow on the way, and the cow was hit with a kill shot that allowed only two steps before she fell forward on her chin and dropped. The movement of the bull had not alarmed the herd, but when the cow dropped, the herd bull pushed the rest of the cow elk away from the downed animals and back to the edge of the trees, exactly as Tate expected. Within moments he heard the blast of a Hawken and knew Maggie had taken her shot; he was certain another elk had fallen. The rifle shot startled the herd and the animals, now somewhat confused, scattered away from the trees and down the long slope toward the brush by the stream in the valley bottom.

It was a family project to field dress the three elk, and it was dusk when they rode back into the clearing with the cabin, with all the horses well loaded. Tate had to use Shady as a packhorse and led the group on foot, but he was pleased with their bounty, confident they had more than enough for the winter. He knew the next few days would be busy with cutting, smoking and wrapping the quarters with muslin and hanging them in the cool cavern behind the cabin. But this was the kind of work they were used to and he was thankful they would be well supplied.

———

20 OCTOBER, 1848 - *We are finally on our way. The past three weeks have been like a whirlwind with the many tasks necessary for our journey. We departed St. Louis 3 October aboard the steamer and made good time up the Missouri. We disembarked 8 October near Westport. My beloved Jessie will return to St. Louis*

with a heavy heart. Our only child, an infant yet, passed from this world just two days into our trip. I am certain his death and the ill health of my beloved are due to the ordeal of the court-martial trial. It has been wearisome indeed, but I am more determined to make this expedition a great success in spite of the naysayers.

I charged Alexis Godey and Edward Kern to take as many men as needed and choose a place for the final preparation camp. As expected, after securing several mounts, they moved south of Westport and set up camp on Boone Creek. We were successful in procuring all the horses and mules necessary, and after sorting and packing our supplies and equipment, we put it all to the test and moved out about five miles and made our first camp on Mission Creek.

I am grateful for the confidence shown by the St. Louis three, Robert Campbell, O.D. Filley, and Thornton Grimsley, who provided the funds and equipment that have made this expedition possible. Although Senator Benton was unsuccessful in gaining the congressional support, I am certain with the success of this venture we will one day see the transcontinental railroad become a reality.

We have thirty-three able men, with many of them experienced on previous expeditions, with skills from artists to doctors and topographers, botanists, millwrights, and military men. I am confident these men will serve honorably and successfully.

I have chosen six men, experienced frontiersmen all, to do the scouting and hunting for this first portion of our journey. Josiah Ferguson, Henry J. Wise, and Thomas Breckenridge are proven Missouri men who were with me on the third expedition, and Raphael Proue, Vincent Tabeau, and Antoine Morin are voyageurs that have also proven themselves with me before. Tomorrow will be the first full day of our journey, and I am expecting great things.

--John Charles Fremont

CHAPTER TWELVE
FALL

MAGGIE LED THE BAY WITH SEAN SITTING ASTRADDLE, AND Tate led the piebald. Both horses were pulling a pair of logs they snaked from the thicker woods and they would cut and split them for firewood. This was to be the last trip into the far woods as winter had already threatened with an early snowfall. Sean twisted around, "Pa, can I hep cut the wood?" Sean had watched his Pa cut and split several logs already and had been kept safely out of the way by his mother. But Tate knew the boy's insistence and desire to be like his dad and had fashioned his son a tomahawk just his size.

"Well, Little Bear, you could probably help me cut some up with your new tomahawk."

The boy grinned and looked down at his mother, walking beside the head of the packhorse, "Ya hear Ma? Pa said I could hep!"

"Well, maybe so now that you have your new tomahawk and all. I suppose it'd be alright."

The woodpile had grown considerably and now was almost as big as the cabin. Tate had explained it was better to have too much than not enough. Maggie always appreciated his protective nature and glanced back over her shoulder to flash her man a smile. She had a secret she was keeping, not wanting to share until she was absolutely certain, and it was just the right time. She was looking forward to the winter and their time together in the cabin. The previous winters had been special times of learning and sharing. Tate never missed an opportunity to procure books of any kind, and their library was growing. The long cold days were made all the warmer by time spent instructing Sean, and learning by teaching. While Tate had been well schooled by his teacher father, Maggie's childhood had little schooling. Because of that lack, she was determined that her children would have the best education possible, and Tate was an excellent teacher.

Once back in the clearing, Tate made short work of derigging the horses and putting them in the corral. He looked at the lean to and his supply of grass and grain and thought if the weather permitted, he might try to get some more pasture grass cut and stacked. He turned away from the corral to see Buster running Lobo into the trees, but knew they would soon be coming back, probably with Lobo doing the chasing. The best friends, bear and wolf, were rarely separated and always playing.

The afternoon was a busy one, with Tate and Maggie using the two-man buck saw to cut the logs to length for Tate to split. While Maggie rested on the porch, Tate busied himself splitting the lengths and Sean used his tomahawk to break branches. He proudly held up the mangled branches, "See Ma, I'se splittin' too!"

"Yes, you are! That's a good job you're doin' too, Little Bear."

The boy beamed at the praise and his mother's use of his new Indian name. He pounded away at the sticks, turning big sticks into little sticks and making the kindling for starting fires. Maggie smiled with pride at her boy and thought what it might be like to have a little girl.

————

7 NOVEMBER, 1848 *Two weeks on the trail along the Kansas River, some call the Kaw, and the Smoky Hill fork. I preferred the timbered country to protect from snowstorms, but the weather has been fair. Had some rain, but upon reaching the Wakarusa, stopped and visited the Pottawattamie Mission. Bad prairie fire but benefitted with plentiful venison and wild turkeys. Crossed the Smoky Hill and were surrounded by herds of buffalo. Took some bulls, but the meat was tough. The cows were tender and tasty. Our Delaware scouts left us, but we continue on our way. This is not unfamiliar country, and I am certain we will reach the Arkansas soon. Edward Kern delighted by the image of the buffalo in the driving snow, but the rest of the men only want to eat them, snow or no snow.*

Now into the bare plains and no shelter from the driving snow. At first light, the temperature was 12 degrees and changed little throughout the day. Have taken a compass reading and am determined to make the Arkansas River.

It was a tiring march of forty miles, but we have come to the Arkansas. Although the cold and snow have been significant, we have been fortunate not to encounter any hostiles. The men have proven themselves hardy and dependable. It is a good group, and all have been diligent in their duties. This is indeed a promising endeavor.

15 NOVEMBER, 1848 *After reaching the river, temperature at sunrise, 18º, came upon a large band of Kiowas. Indians have many horses and mules to trade but want silver for them. Kern pointed out the ornaments made from the silver dollars. It appears* *they pound them out into large discs and braid them into their hair. Have no need of more horses or mules, but the Kiowas continue to follow and have become a nuisance. We camped on Choteau island before going to Big Timbers.*

Met Agent Thomas Fitzpatrick and Doctor Kern mixed some medicines for the Indians. The following day the Indians wanted to trade three mules for more medicines, and Doctor Kern obliged them.

Continued up the Arkansas and crossed the Purgatory fork before stopping opposite Bent's Fort. It is here I hope to find Kit Carson and have him guide us on the rest of our journey. Will also post letters to the Senator and my beloved Jessie.

-- John Charles Fremont

CHAPTER THIRTEEN
GUIDES

"I LOVE THIS KIND OF SNOW," SAID MAGGIE AS SHE SAT IN THE rocker on their porch. The big flakes drifted slowly to the ground and the distant sun, hidden behind the storm clouds, still glared enough light for the flakes to sparkle as they fell. The big ponderosas that circled the clearing were humbled with the heavy snow and hung their branches to display the deep blankets of white. The only sound was the far-off crackling of the snapping of heavy laden branches buckling under winter's weight. Both Maggie and Tate held their cups of steaming coffee, Maggie with both hands and Tate one-handed as he looked at Sean's heavy-lidded eyes that told of his soon coming venture into the land of dreams.

"It is beautiful and something that I will never tire of enjoying," answered the man of the wilderness. He remembered many winters since his first in the mountains. It was in this same cabin that he lasted his first winter after the advice and counsel of his friend and mentor, Kit Carson. He knew if it hadn't been for Kit, he probably would have perished for lack of preparation. But the cautions of his friend bid him to prepare well and because he was wise enough to heed the advice of the experienced mountain man, he prevailed through his first winter and many more since. As he looked around, he drew in a deep breath, content with the preparations for this winter. The stock had plenty of hay and grain, firewood aplenty was stacked nearby, and the cavern held enough meat for two winters. Yes, this would be a comfortable time, he mused to himself.

Sean kicked and startled Tate, but the boy quickly relaxed and dropped back into his deep slumber. Tate smiled at Maggie, "I think he musta had himself a dream. Probably wrestlin' with Buster or Lobo or sumpin'."

Buster the bear had found himself winter quarters in the small offshoot cavern that had its own entrance back in the trees at the far edge of the overhang that sheltered the cabin. They knew they probably would not see him until early spring as he had settled in for his long winter's nap. Lobo seemed a little lost without his playmate, but when he tried to roust the bear, Buster sent him packing with a hefty slap and Lobo got the message. The big wolf lay at the feet of Tate and had joined Sean in dreamland, evidenced by his occasional whimper and jerking of his legs. Tate looked at the wolf and said, "And I think that one is probably chasing a jackrabbit through the snow, the way he's kickin' and such."

Maggie looked at the restless but sleeping Lobo and grinned. "I think he doesn't know how to be still. Even when he's sleepin' he's up to somethin'.

And I've been thinkin', didn't you say your family used to have a special day just to give thanks? I think you said you usually did it after the first snow?"

"Yeah, we did. Pa taught us about the pilgrims and their hard times and how they never ceased to give thanks for all the Lord had done for them. He used to call it a day of thanksgiving, and he said most folks had kinda made it a special time in November. We used to make up a big dinner, invite folks over and such. Is that what you're thinkin'?"

"Well, I don't think we can invite folks over, but it would be nice to do something like that," answered Maggie, wishing there was some way to have more of a festive day.

"Alright, how would you like a turkey for dinner?"

She looked at Tate with surprise written across her face, "You mean it? You could get us a turkey?"

"Maybe. Usually they're gone further south by now, but I've been hearin' some gobblin' down by the crick the last couple days, and there just might be one or two left behind," answered Tate, looking at his wife with a sly grin. He knew exactly where the gobblers had been nesting and he was certain he could get at least one.

LOBO LED the way as the two made their way from the trees that draped from the long line of mountains like ruffled skirts from a pirouetting young maiden falling in folds along the ridge tops. The tree line stopped, abruptly giving way to the snow-covered grassy slopes as fringe from the hem of the maiden's garment to be adorned with the edging of willows and alder brush along the creek bank. It was in that brush that Tate expected to find the turkeys. Once at the edge of the bushes, he dropped to his knees with Lobo on his stomach at his side and gave his mimic of the turkey's gobble. Almost instantly, he was answered, not once but twice.

He held Maggie's bow with arrow nocked. He had chosen her smaller bow as opposed to his longbow because her's was the shorter style used by the plains Indian and more suited for close-in hunting. Tate rose to one knee, the other leg stretched out before him, and stayed motionless and quiet, waiting. The chuckling of the stream, with ice along the edges was the only sound to be heard. There was no wind to stir the willows and the songbirds stayed in their shelters, a good sign of another coming storm. After a few moments of silence, Tate turned his head toward the stream and gave another challenging gobble. It too was answered, and Tate waited. Within moments, a long-bearded gobbler cautiously walked from the brush, searching for his challenger. Tate drew back and let the arrow fly to its mark. The narrow-point buried itself in the chest of the bird just in front of its wing. A flutter of feathers and a slight choking sound was all that heralded the sacrifice of the big grey-feathered bird. Lobo sprang from his spot beside his master and was instantly on the bird, but a simple "no" from Tate stayed the wolf from attacking the carcass. Tate picked up the big turkey, pleased at the heft of it, and looking at Lobo said, "This is gonna make mighty fine eatin', and best of all, it's gonna make Maggie mighty happy too!"

As they neared the clearing and the cabin, Lobo stopped suddenly and with lowered head, let a low rumbling growl come from deep within. Tate froze, then dropped into a crouch to peer through the trees and saw three horses, tethered at the corral fence. There was no movement, no sound, no reason for alarm, but Lobo slowly moved forward, eyes searching. Tate was at his side and had nocked an arrow in readiness as he stepped cautiously. They stayed within the cover of the trees, circling to the side of the cabin to approach along the cliff wall and overhang. As they neared, a familiar voice said, "It is good that you return, Longbow. Your friends have come to visit you, and you were not here."

Tate relaxed and replaced the arrow in the quiver before stepping from the side of the cabin to see White Feather grinning at his approach. "Ahh, but I am here now, and it is good to see our friends. But you are not alone White Feather, who is with you?"

Raven and Red Blossom came from the cabin to stand

beside Raven's sister, White Feather. "Is that all you bring? What kind of a feast will that be to welcome your friends?" asked a grinning Raven, pointing at the feathered bundle on Tate's back.

"Hah! This bird is more than enough for a skinny Comanche like you!" declared Tate as he mounted the steps to greet his friends. The men clasped forearms and hugged one another, slapping each other on the back as Lobo took his place on the porch beside the rockers.

Maggie called from within the cabin, "If you got that turkey, you need to get it ready to roast!" White Feather and Red Blossom laughed as they returned to the cabin, leaving the men to their task of preparing the bird and the pit for the roasting. It was the fulfillment of Maggie's wishing to have good friends for their feast of thanksgiving.

————

"WELL, if I hadn't seen it with my own eyes, I wouldn'ta believed it. John Fremont, what are you doin' here at this time o' year?" asked William Bent as he watched Fremont tether his horse at the rail outside the sutler's store. "I mean, not that I ain't glad to see ya' n' all, but if you hadn't noticed, it's gettin' to be winter time, and that's when you're s'posed to be holed up with yore honey in some nice warm cottage in the city!"

Fremont chuckled at the greeting of his friend as he extended his hand to shake. "I come lookin' for Carson, he around?"

"No, no, he's got more sense. He's got him a wife, and last I heard he's doin' what you should be doin'. Probably sittin' in a rockin' chair in a nice warm house down in Taos." The disappointment was evident on Fremont's face as Bent continued. "Why, what'chu lookin' fer him for?"

"We've got another expedition. I'm lookin' to find a route for the railroad!" he declared proudly. "And I'm needin' a guide to get us through the mountains. We had some Delaware doing the scouting for us, but they left. So, you wouldn't happen to know where we could find one, do you?"

Bent looked at the explorer with his head cocked to the side, measuring his resolve, and said, "Just might, just might. Foller me," he said as he started off for the game room on the upper floor of the corner cabin. The two men mounted the steep stairs and entered the smoke-filled room, and Bent led the way to a big corner table where several men were playing cards. As they approached, the men, all dressed in buckskins and looking every bit the mountain men they were, looked at Bent and his follower.

"Fellas, I want'chu to meet somebody," and turned to motion Fremont forward, placed his hand on his shoulder and said, "This hyars the Pathfinder hisself, John Fremont!"

Fremont extended his hand to shake with the men as Bent introduced each one. "This is Joe Walker, and George Nidever there. The fella in the corner thar is Antoine Leroux and this'ns Wooton, most folks call him Uncle Dick Wooton." Bent looked at each of the men and said, "Fremont's lookin' fer a guide to get his expedition 'crost the mountains. Any you fellers int'ersted?"

Each of the men looked at Fremont, considering, and the man responded, "We're looking to find a route for a railroad. There are several investors that believe we can get a railroad all the way from the Mississippi to the Pacific coast and I believe we can find the route. You will be well paid for your services."

Antoine Leroux looked up from his cards and asked, "How come they call you the Pathfinder, seein's how you have to have a guide to show you the path?"

The others chuckled at the remark, each one thinking

much the same. Joe Walker said, "Seems to me it'd be best done in the summer. There's gonna be too much snow in the mountains this time a'year." The men at the table and Bent all nodded their head in agreement as they looked at Fremont.

"I crossed the Sierra Nevadas in the winter time, and I believe we can cross the Rockies as well. It is important we find a route that can be used year-round and the only way we can do that is to make the expedition in the winter. We are well equipped and supplied. We have thirty-three able-bodied and experienced men, good men all, and I'm certain we can do it. But we need a man that knows the mountains."

The men looked at one another, none anxious to leave the warmth of the fort, but Uncle Dick Wooton folded his cards and slowly stood, "I might give it a try. Ain't doin' nuthin' but losin' here, so, might's well get sumpin' fer my troubles."

"Good, good. How about the rest of you men? We could use another man?" asked Fremont, but there were no other takers. Wooton came around the table, and as the three men started down the stairs, Uncle Dick said, "There's another fella we might get. Old Bill Williams is up at that tradin' post at where Fountain Creek hits the Arkansas. We might get him to come along, he knows the country better'n anybody."

CHAPTER FOURTEEN
HARDSCRABBLE

THE RISING SUN PAINTED THE DISTANT MOUNTAINS; PIKE'S Peak to the northwest and the Spanish Peaks to the south, both capped with a fresh coat of snow, a blushing pink. With the sun at their backs and the temperature a chilly 10^0, Uncle Dick Wooton started the expedition following the Arkansas River. He had suggested they try to get Old Bill Williams to join them and he would be found at the trader's fort of Pueblo. The seventy-five miles from Bent's Fort was covered in two and a half days, and this day had turned warmer with a bright sun and clear blue sky. Fremont took it as a good omen, and he expected the rest of the journey to be no more difficult than what they had already experienced.

"Ho! Old Bill! You ol' scalawag! You plannin' on spendin' yore sunset years sittin' in this God-forsaken place? Wheeeeoooooo, it stinks in hyar!" declared Uncle Dick as he pushed through the door of the little adobe structure. He tripped over a pair of piglets that raced to the open door chased by a squawking goose. Wooton pressed himself against the wall to let the menagerie escape as he looked through the low cloud of smoke that bent the rays of sunlight struggling to get through the fly-specked window. Three men were seated at a round table near the window, using the only light to see the spots on the worn-out cards they were using. One man, long and lanky with grey whiskers that hid his neck and face, squinted at the noisy newcomer and said, "Wal, bust my britches if it ain't Uncle Dick! C'mon o'er hyar and sit a spell. Mebbe you can convince that ornery clerk to break out a jug, our credit's shot!"

Wooton motioned to the clerk and walked to the table as Old Bill Williams stood stoop-shouldered and ducking his head to avoid the low timbers in the roof to extend his hand to his friend. "Uncle Dick, don' know if you know these fellers but this hyar," motioning to the man to his right, "is Lucien Maxwell, and that'ns Dick Owens, and I think you know Zenas Leonard thar."

"Howdy fellers. You too, Zenas. Long time no see, been stayin' outta trouble?" The well-known mountain man nodded his head and looked for the spittoon to relieve himself of a mouthful of tobacco. He looked at Wooton, "What brings you thisaway?"

"Oh, I hooked up with a fella name o' Fremont. He's wantin' to cross them mountains an' needs somebody to show him the way." Wooton noticed the men looking past him to the door that creaked open and turned to see Fremont coming through. "Thar he is now." He looked to Fremont, motioned him to join them, "Fellas, this hyar is John Fremont. Some folks, mostly them newspapers back East, have taken to callin' him the Pathfinder. He's wantin' to find a route fer the railroad." Wooton looked to Old Bill and added, "And we was thinkin' you might wanna come along."

The four men let out a collective, "Whooooeeee!" and clamored about how the mountains was no place to be in the middle of winter. "Sides, everythin' we see is tellin' us this'ns gonna be a bad'n," said Zenas. He was a man well-traveled in the mountains and his advice based on many years of experience, was respected.

Fremont spoke up and echoed his remark about crossing the Sierra Nevadas. "What is needed, is a route that can be used year-round and to find that, we must make the crossing in the winter."

"You mean, try to make the crossing. I've been where you wanna go, and I'm here to tell you there ain't no railroad gonna make it cross them mountains in the winter. Why, them mountains get upwards o' twenty feet, and they hold onto it till late spring. Nosir, ain't no country fer no railroad," declared Maxwell, shaking his head.

"Well, how 'bout it, Old Bill? You gonna let these fireplace prophets keep you from another adventure?" asked Wooton.

Old Bill, still standing, lifted his foot to rest on the seat of the chair and he leaned down to rest his elbow on the uplifted knee, setting his chin in his hand. He looked around at the others, knowing the truth of their warnings, but when he looked at the expectant faces of Fremont and Wooton, he let a grin slowly cross his face, "Why not? It's gettin' plum boring around here, an' worse, I'm startin' to smell like the rest o' these animals!" He looked again at Fremont, held out his hand and said, "Shore, I'll go."

28 NOVEMBER, 1848 *William Sherley "Old Bill" Williams is proving his worth. Two days out of Pueblo we came to the village of Hardscrabble. Former army officer, Lancaster Lupton, bid us welcome and for two days we feasted on chicken, baked squash, milk, and beans. These former fur traders now turned farmers had an abundance of corn. We shelled and sacked 130 bushels to take with us for the stock.*

The afternoon of the 25th we started up Hardscrabble creek in fine weather. Yesterday we had difficult going through a deep canyon that brought us higher and into the snow. We camped in the aspen in three feet of snow. This morning, we came into a wide and beautiful valley with the Sangre de Cristo mountains looking like a palisade with the snow-covered peaks. Williams assures me there is a pass at the lower end of the valley. This valley is covered with deep snow, and the men are all afoot, the animals loaded with the much-needed corn. We hope to reach the pass and cross over into what Williams calls the San Luis Valley. Hopefully, the weather will improve soon.

--John C. Fremont

"THERE SHE BE!" declared Williams as Fremont and Wooton rode up beside him. He was pointing to the winding Huer-fano creek, mostly iced over, in the bottom of the valley. He pointed to the aspen in the notch of the mountains, "And that's whar we be goin'!"

Fremont stood in his stirrups, shaded his eyes from the bright glare of the sun reflecting off the snow, and looked at the mountains. He pointed to a cut between the towering peaks, "Is that where the pass crosses?" Charles Preuss, the topographer, was beside Fremont and looked to the moun-tains, shaking his head at the wonder.

Williams and Wooton looked where Fremont pointed, "Yup, shore 'nuff. It ain't too bad a climb, but that snow's mighty deep!"

"Well, let's get going then," ordered Fremont. But an approaching rider, waving his arms, stopped them.

Josiah Ferguson, one of the Missouri frontiersman, reined his mount beside Fremont, "Sir, one o' the mules broke loose an' the men are chasin' it down. The others are tangled up an' it's gonna take a while 'fore we can get movin'!"

Fremont dropped his head, shaking it side to side, then

lifted it to look at Ferguson. "Alright Josiah, let me know when everything's ready."

The crossing of the pass would prove more challenging than expected. Williams repeatedly asked himself what he was doing with this bunch. He looked back along the line of men and mules struggling through the deep snow and biting wind. The first day's progress was only three miles, and he knew they would be lucky to make eight miles today. When they were in the thick timber, they were protected from the wind, but the drifted snow was often armpit deep, and the men had to alternate turns at breaking trail.

When the grey light of early morning pried their eyes open, Williams and Wooton were covered with almost half two feet of fresh snow. Throwing the blankets aside and stomping their feet to bring circulation, the men looked at one another, asking the same silent question as to why they were here. With Old Bill leading, the expedition crossed the summit at 9,772 feet and had their first view of the broad valley and the distant San Juan mountains. The descent of the pass proved even more difficult, with downed timber and drifted snow, but before the day's end, they were at the foot of the range and on the edge of the sand dunes.

CHAPTER FIFTEEN
COMPANY

"I'M TELLIN' YA, YORE CRAZIER'N A MOONSHINE DRINKIN' potlikker if you think you can make it crost them mountains in this kinda weather!" shouted Uncle Dick Wooton. He had been arguing with Fremont about the futility of continuing into the mountains. Convinced the weather would make any further progress impossible and that lives would be lost, Wooton was doing all he could to convince the stubborn Fremont to turn back. He waved his arms in the air in frustration and turned to Williams, "Old Bill, you know I'm right! Tell this crazy galoot he's dummer'n a one-eyed mule with a broke leg and the mule'd have a better chance than that stiff-necked pilgrim!" He spat the words through the icicles hanging from his moustache. "Look at them mules! You cain't see'm fer the icicles! They look like they's already froze!"

Old Bill stood with his long Kentucky rifle butt on his foot and leaning on the muzzle as he listened to the rampaging Wooton. "Uncle Dick, we signed on to take these fellers across them mountains," motioning with his arm sweeping toward the west, "an' we're honor bound to do that," he drawled.

"Honor! Ain't no honor in freezin' to death cuz o' some dumb hair brained scheme thought up some fat politicians sittin' by a warm fireplace in their big house back east. If they wants to cross these mountains in the snow, then let 'em get off their kiesters an' buck trail for us!" Wooton stomped around in a small circle, restoring circulation in his cold feet. He looked at Fremont and with his icicle crusted beard bouncing with every word he declared, "I'm goin' back an' if any o' these fellers got a lick a sense, they'd come with me!"

In a calm but firm voice, Fremont responded, "Dick, if you want to go, then go. And if any of these men are refusing to go on with the expedition, they can go with you. I'll not cut into our supplies for any of you quitters, you'll have to make it on your own." He dropped his head and turned to Old Bill. "Shall we continue?"

When Wooton started back up the difficult pass, three others were with him. Elijah Andrews, who had tried this journey for the adventure, chose to return to his father who had dropped out at Pueblo. Billy Bacon and Benjamin Beadle, both of Missouri, also decided Wooton was right and to turn back was the wise choice. With a two day stop at Hardscrabble, the four men were soon safe and away from the mountains and the bitter winter.

Old Bill led out, riding a sure-footed big mule, but the wind had blown the snow free of the sandhills and stacked it deep in the narrow valley between the sand and the timbered flank of the mountains. The mule humped his back and jumped into the three-foot-deep snow drifts, and at Bill's urging continued his humping and jumping for a consider-able distance. When Bill tried to lift the mule's head for one more jump, the big jack shook his head and almost pulled the reins from Bill's hands. He motioned to the tree line for the others to work their way into the shelter of the pines and once free of the drift, Bill joined them.

"We best make camp here, we ain't gettin' anywhere, and the animals are already tuckered out," explained Bill, speaking to Fremont.

"You're right of course. Maybe with a good meal and a good night's rest here in the trees, we can do better tomorrow," answered Fremont.

But the night would not be as restful as they hoped. A bitter wind whistled through the pines, and another foot of snow fell on the tired travelers. Once the snow stopped, the temperature dropped, and by first light, Fremont saw the thermometer read 0^0. But his determination rolled him from his blankets and roused the men. After a few cups of hot java, they pushed north. Putting Alexis Godey, an experienced frontiersman on par with Williams, in charge of the main group, Fremont, Preuss, Lorenzo Vincenthaler and Old Bill branched off to explore what appeared to be another pass back over the Sangres. Ever hopeful of finding a crossing suitable for the railroad, Fremont was once again disappointed by the steep grade and narrow passage of the pass that would later become known as Medano pass.

As the four returned on the descent of the pass toward the dunes, Old Bill was in the lead and was suddenly stopped by the big mule with his ears pointed forward. Standing in the trail was a bearded man with a red and black capote, hood up over his fur cap, and Hawken rifle held loosely at his side. The man didn't move nor say a word, and Old Bill spoke, "Where did you come from?"

A simple, almost imperceptible nod toward the uphill side of the trail was the only answer given. Bill leaned forward and shaded his eyes from the bright sun reflecting off the snow and said, "Say, ain't you that feller I met in Bent's Fort? By gum, you are, Saint, Tate Saint!"

"Got some hot coffee in the cabin yonder," replied Tate with a nod in the direction of his cabin. "Trail turns just past the scrub oak," another nod down the trail to indicate the turn-off.

Bill looked beyond the man, and turned to speak to Fremont, "Whatchu think?"

"Sounds mighty good to me!" answered Fremont.

Bill turned around, and there was no one there. Tate had disappeared into the trees as quickly and quietly as he came. Bill dug heels into the mule and pushed on down the descent, almost missed the smaller trail, covered with fresh snow and no tracks, and led the group of four into the trees. When they came into the clearing, Tate was standing on the porch and motioned for them to tether their animals at the corral fence and come inside.

The four men stomped their feet clear of snow and filed into the warm cabin. Maggie was at the counter, arms crossed before her, but she smiled a welcome, and the introductions followed. The four men stood before the fireplace, hands outstretched as Bill spoke, "I never expected to see anybody livin' up here. How long you folks been here?"

"Built the cabin goin' on six years ago, but family's been here more'n three."

"So, you know this country very well?" asked Fremont.

"You might say so," answered Tate.

"Well, Mr. Saint, we need another guide to get us across those mountains," stated Fremont, pointing to the west and indicating the distant San Juans.

"And just why do you want to cross those mountains at this time of year?"

Fremont began explaining the purpose of the expedition, adding his experience in the Sierra Nevadas and the need for the year-round route. "So, you see our need of someone that's very familiar with the mountains."

Tate looked at Old Bill with raised eyebrows, and the long tall mountain man shrugged his shoulders and dropped his eyes. Tate looked at Fremont then at Maggie whose expression was somber and unchanging. "You're asking me to leave my family and go out into this weather to try to get you over mountains that shouldn't be tried in the winter just because you want to bring a railroad through here?"

"That's about it," answered Fremont. "There's half a million square miles out there that could provide homes for thousands of people. Land that needs to be settled and a nation that needs to grow. And it will take a railroad to do that and I believe the good Lord brought us to this point to meet you because we need you to guide us."

Tate looked at Old Bill again and asked, "What do you think about this scheme?"

"Son, I gave up thinkin' when I weren't much older'n you. After I spent my time preachin' to the Osage and translatin' God's Word into their language, I decided my thinkin' days were over. Now I leave all that to you young'uns."

"They're," motioning to Fremont, "wantin' to take all this land away from the natives, fill it with farmers and cities and ruin everything!"

Old Bill nodded his head in agreement, "But it's what they call progress, and I done found out that ya' cain't stop progress."

"I believe my father would call you a philosopher," drawled Tate. He looked at Maggie who shrugged her shoulders passing the decision back to him. He turned to Fremont, "Tell ya' what. Your men are camped down below, and if I'm goin' with you, I'll be there at first light. But,

I'm only doin' it to prove to you it can't be done, and you can't bring a railroad through those mountains."

Fremont grinned and extended his hand to Tate, "Fine, fine. I believe you're just what we need. Now I know we can do it!"

Tate shook the man's hand as he shook his head,

wondering what he just got himself into, as he walked over to stand beside Maggie. He slipped an arm around her shoulders and pulled her to him, letting the closeness explain his decision. She knew her man and knew he could not let these men wander into the snow-covered mountains without his help.

CHAPTER SIXTEEN
RIO GRANDE

IT WAS THE KIND OF NIGHT THAT THOSE OF THE MOUNTAINS knew would be trying. The dark sky was clear and bedecked with a myriad of stars. The wideband that marked the angelic Milkyway arched overhead as the expedition hunkered down in their blankets. Several had risen to feed the fire and find some comfort from the flames while wrapped in their blankets beside the brilliant markers of their camp. Those that had put pine boughs down to separate them from the snow shivered as they drew their legs up in a futile effort to hide from the lances of cold that pierced their covers. Mules and horses crowded together to find warmth with one another and the pines crackled as what little moisture was held in their branches froze and split the boughs with a snapping that echoed through the forest. Mumbles and curses replaced the usual snoring as the men fought against the invisible foe of the darkness. The numbers surrounding the campfires doubled as most had surrendered any thought of sleep.

Dr. Kern stood with blankets wrapped around his shoulders and pulled up behind his head and with icicles in his whiskers, he chattered as he exclaimed, "Th . . th. . . this ish the m. . . m . . .most h.. . h . . .horribly un . . .un . . uncom . . .fortable night of m. . . m . . my life!"

Grunts and attempted amens echoed his chattered words as others stomped their feet and struggled against the miserable cold. They looked back up the mountainside, hoping to see the sunrise, but old sol wouldn't make his face seen for several more hours. And all the men agreed they were the most miserable hours they had spent so far in their lives.

MAGGIE STOOD with Sean at her side and Lobo lying at her feet as she watched Tate mount Shady and turn to leave the clearing. After his early breakfast, the two had prayer together, and she elicited a promise that he would do his best to be back by Christmas. "That should be plenty of time for them pilgrims. The way I figger it, it'll take a couple days to get to the foothills yonder, another week to get 'em through to the other side, dependin' of course on the weather an' such, and another week to get me home. So, I should be back by Christmas."

"If you don't, you'll be sorry!" she declared. "I don't know what I'll do, but you'll be payin' for it a long time," she vowed as a slow grin crossed her face.

"Well, darlin', you should be fine. You've got plenty o' food and firewood, and there's books galore for you and Sean to explore. You just keep your Hawken loaded and by the door, and you won't have any problems, I'm sure." He looked down at Sean and said, "And you take care of your ma, now, y'hear?"

"I will Pa, I will," answered the tyke.

He turned in his saddle, and she waved at her man. He waved back and started from the clearing in the direction of the camp below the trees. When he rode into the group, Fremont asked him to join him by the fire. Beside Fremont were Williams and two other salty looking men that eyed the new addition with a little disdain. When Tate stood beside Fremont, the man began, "Williams here thinks we should go further south and follow the Rio Grande into the mountains. He says there's a pass, known as Leroux pass there that will take us over the mountains and to the valley of the Gunnison which runs into the Colorado. And Old Bill also told of another pass farther north called the little Cochetopa that crosses over. So, what do you think?"

Tate looked to Old Bill Williams and knew he was being tested by the man and probably by Fremont as well. He asked Fremont, "Didn't you say you wanted to follow the 38th parallel?"

"Yes, yes I did."

"And didn't you say the 38th lay north of where we are now? And doesn't it lay directly across this valley from about there to there?" He had pointed out the obvious landmarks for the parallel.

"Yes, that what Preuss said, the 38th is about 10 miles north of where we are now."

"Well, the little Cochetopa is about another 10 miles north of that and moves to the northwest from there. Now the Rio Grande is about 20 miles south of here. The pass that Leroux spoke of runs almost due north from the Rio Grande and does come out at the Gunnison a bit farther west from where the Cochetopa comes out. Both of 'em are about 40 miles north of the 38th parallel. So, I guess it's up to you. Do you wanna go well north of the parallel, or do you wanna go south and end up north?"

All of the listeners became restless at the newcomer's explanation and started looking around and shuffling their feet, but they knew he was right. Fremont asked, "Well, do you know of a way that would more closely follow the 38th and bear due west?"

"Not that I know of, cuz the mountains due west o' here," and he pointed to the distant San Juans, "are rougher, higher and more rugged than any others in the Rockies."

"You mean you don't think we can make it through?"

"Ain't that what I said last night?"

Fremont nodded his head and looked around at the others, finally turning back to Tate and asked, "Of these two routes, which do you think would be the easiest?"

"Normally, the northern route would be easier, but what with the snow we been gettin' and prob'ly will get, the southern route's the best." He dropped his head and continued, "'Cep'in, as cold as it's been, there's a point up the river that the canyon narrows, and I don't think we can cross it."

"Why not?" asked a frustrated Fremont.

"As cold as it's been, it'll be iced over, but the river's too swift for it to freeze solid. If you try to cross it, the ice'll give way, and men and animals'll fall through and be dead in minutes."

Fremont looked at the man, then to Williams and the others. He considered Tate's remarks, wondering if they weren't a little biased against the possibility of passage and decided, "We'll go to the Rio Grande and see where it takes us into the mountains. If we need to change our course, so be it, but for now, it's south." The men looked at Fremont then to Tate and Williams motioned for Tate to follow him.

When they were clear of the others, Williams spoke softly, "Tate, this man is determined to get crost them mountains, and if all it took was stubbornness, we wouldn't have any trouble. But, I'm gonna be countin' on you to keep us on the best route, no matter what that pilgrim says, cuz there's a lot o' lives at stake here."

"I understand Bill, but I'm thinkin' you know these mountains as well as I do, so mebbe with two heads together, we might get this thing done an' I can get back home to muh family."

"Alright then," and he looked at the sturdy Morgan bred horse with its shaggy winter coat and asked, "That horse of your'n gonna be alright with breakin' trail?"

Tate nodded his head as he stepped into his saddle. With a bit of knee pressure, Shady stepped out into the bitter cold morning and kicked snow with every step. The frigid temperatures made the fresh snow powdery, and the going was easy as Shady started across the flats of the San Luis Valley.

10 DECEMBER, 1848 *The bitter cold has shown us no mercy. Since leaving Hardscrabble the temperature has hovered around 0, many days well below 0° and everyone has been miserable. The only reason the men and mules keep moving is to have some semblance of warmth. We crossed the wide valley of the San Luis in terrible weather making 22 miles the first day of crossing but when we stopped, there was only greasewood and sage to make our fires and they didn't last the night. The second day was worse with high winds driving the snow and making it almost impossible to see our way. We made another 15 miles and came to the mouth of the canyon of the Rio Grande. The nearby mountains gave some relief from the winds. Today, Tate Saint and Bill Williams brought in some elk that made fine eating and after our feast, we made another five miles before camping for the night. We are running low on our grain supply, with no access to any graze for the animals, have been forced to feed the corn and now in short supply.*

We find ourselves considerably south of the 38th parallel. Preuss used his Astrolabe and Sextant to determine our exact location and as Saint had said, we are over 20 miles south of the 38th.

Am considering finding another route that will take us north and more in line with our goal. If the Lord is willing, and we have better weather tomorrow, perhaps we'll change course.

--- John C. Fremont

"HERE'S WHAT I'M THINKIN'," SAID OLD BILL AS HE SQUATTED next to the fire across from Tate. They were the only two at the small fire made by Tate as he practiced his habit of camping apart from the others. "You're right 'bout that canyon of the Rio Grande up round the bend. Ain't no way we can get past that what with the narrow cut and the froze o'er river, but if'n we go up thar, that stubborn Fremont'd want to try it anyway an' we'd prob'ly lose several men and mules 'fore he'd give in. But, you e'er been up Alder Creek hereabouts?"

"I've done a little huntin' up here a ways," admitted Tate, wondering what conspiratorial plan Williams had up his sleeve.

"Wal, it's been a while fer me, but the best I recollect, if'n we foller this up to the headwaters, it'll put us up top some'ers round the flat top just shy o' Mesa Mountain. When we get thar, then we can see the lay o' the land and mebbe Fremont'll decide whar he wants to go from thar. Cuz, that'd put us not too fer from that pass Laroux was aimin' fer, or we could go on north to the Cochetopa. Either way, it'll get us 'round that narrow canyon o' the Rio Grande."

"That's also Tabeguache or Uncompahgre Ute country. They might not like us comin' into their winter grounds," commented a pensive Tate. He was thinking about his friends among the Ute, Two Eagles and Red Bird, yet he knew they were with the Caputa Ute that stayed farther north.

"I don't think we'll be runnin' into any of 'em up yonder. Them Ute are smarter'n this bunch o' pilgrims, and they'd rather stay in their nice warm wickiups than go trompin' around in the snow," declared Williams. "So, what'chu think?"

"Snows gonna be mighty deep up there, but if we stay to the south-facing slopes where the sun and wind are workin', we could prob'ly make it alright."

"Fine, fine. So, how 'bout you leadin' out in the mornin' an' I'll get these pilgrims movin' an' we'll foller yore sign?"

Tate nodded his head in agreement, poured coffee for the two of them, and they sat staring into the flames, contemplating the morrow's trek.

THE PREVAILING WINDS were from the west and swept over the mountains drifting the snow into the gullies, ravines, and canyons and leaving the mountain tops clear of all but the frozen glaciers that hugged the granite tops and notches. As Tate basked in the early morning sun that shone through the valley of the Rio Grande, he looked to the north and the route chosen by Williams. The narrow valley of Alder Creek was smoothed over with the drifted snow that appeared like the frosted top of a decorated cake. But this was no wedding he was headed for, but a direct assault on the mountains of the San Juans, some of the most rugged mountains in all the Rockies.

He gigged Shady toward the left side of the valley, to a trail that was well up the side slope and often sheltered by the juniper and piñon that clung to the east facing hillside. The Grulla was happy to stretch out on the trail, and Tate breathed deep of the smell of juniper. It was good to be away from the flats with the sage and greasewood, but the mountains would not easily yield to the intruders into the winter wilderness.

It was mid-morning before the sun crested the mountains on the east side of the valley and brought its warmth to the man and his horse. Tate had stopped to give Shady a bit of rest as he sat on the rocks beside the trail, chewing some jerky and looking around. He estimated the snow in the bottom of the narrow valley to be between four and five feet deep, and the farther upstream they moved, the deeper it piled. Even though the winds cleared the hillsides, there were areas where the drifts would pile up behind anything that broke the wind. Tate was looking up the trail at just such a drift that stretched out from a rock formation on the uphill side of the trail, and he could see several others further on.

He stood and stepped up on another boulder to get a look back down the valley. He could barely make out the winding snake of the expedition following his trail and slowly working their way up the wide draw. With the mules on short rations due to the dwindling supply of corn, they would snatch at anything edible along the trail. But those at the end of the line had nothing left to take and walked with heads down and swinging side to side. Tate shook his head and stepped into his saddle to continue up the trail.

Whenever he confronted a drift, he would rein Shady into the trees on the uphill side to circumvent the drift. Within a short while, he came to the fork of three smaller canyons and knew these to be the branches of Alder Creek. He pushed Shady downslope to cross the first fork, aiming to round the point between the west fork and middle fork. As they dropped into the valley bottom, the snow deepened, and Shady struggled for footing. He pushed through the loose snow, fighting to buck the drift. As they neared the bottom, Tate reined up the Grulla to let him catch his wind as he surveyed the drift before him. He looked up the narrow canyon and saw nothing but white, but the contour of the drift and an occasional slump told of the path of the creek, and he followed it down to where they stood. Just in front of them was the bottom of Alder creek, and Tate knew the danger of breaking through the ice to the stream below.

Tate slid from the saddle to stand beside his horse, the snow over his waist. He leaned into the drift, pushing the heavy packed white with his mittened hands side to side and forced each step. He tested his weight with each step before moving any further. The fight with the white sapped his strength and brought sweat as he struggled, but he continued, leading Shady at rein-length behind. He pushed away the snow, lifted his foot and kicked away room for another step. He leaned forward to slap at the drift and heard a cracking sound that he knew was the ice across the creek. He froze, leaning back to shift his weight. He paused, caught his breath, and began shoveling the snow away with his hands and kicking at it as he had room. When he had the snow piled to each side, he tested the ice again. It held. He gingerly moved to the end of his cleared path and continued his fight with the drift. Stopping often for short rests, he finally cleared enough to allow Shady room to cross and if necessary, make it to the far bank.

He walked back to the horse, stroked his head as he talked to his friend, and stepped out, reins in hand. With the loose snow still almost knee deep, he cautiously led the horse as he walked almost sideways, watching each step of the animal. Suddenly the cracking of the ice startled both man and horse, and Tate leaned back into the snow to pull at the reins and bridle of Shady. The horse had thrown his head up as his hooves slipped on the cracking ice and with one mighty lunge, he landed on the far bank with one hoof on either side of Tate, now on his back in the snow looking up at the wide-eyed Shady. He started laughing as he struggled out from between the legs of his friend and stood beside him, stroking his neck and talking into his ear as he said, "What a friend you are, why, if you'da been one o' them lop-eared mules, you'da landed smack dap in the middle o' me. Thanks, buddy, I won't forget this."

Once they cleared the drift in the bottom, Tate worked out the trail they would follow to climb the mountains before them. He rounded the point between the forks and took to the easy slope that turned back to follow the west fork of the Alder. It was an easy climb and afforded him a good view back down the valley to see the long line of mules and men winding their way up the trail. He stopped near a cluster of juniper and let Shady crop some of the bunch grass that was clear of the snow. He sat on a sun-warmed rock and munched on some stale cornbread and buffalo jerky as he watched the slow progress of the mule train.

He soon stood and looked up the long slope and planned the best route to ascend the mountain. He used his brass telescope to search the hillside and tree line for a possible camp for the night and spotted a reasonably level site just below the tree line. Putting away the scope, he took another look below at the expedition, saw they were crossing the creek and noted they had broken through the ice, but managed to cross the bottom without any evident problems. He looked back up the hill and muttered a short prayer, *Lord, we're sure gonna need you to help us on this one.*"

CHAPTER EIGHTEEN
CLIMBING

TATE WATCHED AS THE MULE TRAIN FILED INTO THE CAMPSITE clearing. The mules were staggering, the men stumbling, and most would fall or sit down as soon as they stopped. The temperature was dropping and the wind increasing as it cut across the flat that held the camp nestled against the trees. He noticed some of the mules were overloaded and was told it was because of the mules that had given out and were left beside the trail to feed the buzzards. He looked down the long slope and saw where the mules had fallen, but the cold had kept what buzzards remained in their protected lairs, and the sky was empty.

Fires began to blossom, and the men stirred towards the warmth. Jackson Saunders, the personal chef and orderly of Fremont busied himself preparing the remains of the elk meat for Fremont while others made do with some elk and having a go at the first mule steaks of the journey. Saunders was the free negro servant of the Bentons' that had come along at Jessie's insistence to take care of her husband. He was a sturdy, well-built man and under other circumstances would probably have been a fine field hand, but the man was an inspiration to all that came to know him as his spirit never waned, and he continually praised his Lord.

As is true with every venture involving many men, they began to group up, with the Kern brothers, Preuss the topographer, and Godey usually gathering near Fremont. Lorenzo Vincenthaler, a strong personality, and outspoken man, seemed to gather others that leaned toward the opposing opinion or complainers like Micajah McGehee of Mississippi who came along for the adventure, Charles Taplin and Henry King, both members of previous expeditions, and Thomas Martin, another veteran of other expeditions. Others, mostly craftsmen in their own right, like Henry Rohrer, a millwright, and Joseph Stepperfelodt, a gunsmith, seemed to bond together and had a spirit of hard work. Several Frenchman, Raphael Proue, Vincent Tabeau, and Antoine Morin, naturally camped together, as did the three California Indians, Manuel, Joaquin, and Gregorio. Most of the others showed no preference and seemed to get along with everyone.

With Fremont a strong authoritarian, most of the men yielded to his command and experience and followed instructions without complaint and the work of the expedition was readily accomplished.

When the first light of morning started the camp stirring, the men were greeted with fresh snowfall that covered their blankets, making most hesitant to come from the warmth of their bedrolls. But the banging of pots and pans and the crackling of fresh-stoked fires rousted the men and stirred the animals.

Tate had already started on the trail, knowing this day would not be an easy one. The wind howled down the canyon, carrying much of the new fallen snow and piling it at every dip or notch. The trail held to the steep slope of the mountain and overlooked the narrow canyon below. With the wind moving downslope, the snow naturally dropped on the shelf of the trail and began to pile up, making the path almost impassable. Tate stepped down from Shady and began kicking his way through the drift, only to have the wind fill his tracks behind him. The hood of his capote kept the snow from his neck, but the wind cut against his face like millions of tiny daggers. He pulled his scarf up to cover his face and pulled the fur cap down to partially shield his eyes, but the fur caught the snow, and his hot breath soon turned the snow to ice, and he was continually slapping his face to free the icicles that threatened to blind him.

He looked back at Shady, following with head down to avoid the wind, as he saw the icicles building up in the horse's mane and over his heavy winter coat. Tate turned and tried to free the hair of the icicles and crusted snow, then tired, he sat down in the snow beside the trail, putting his elbows to his knees to rest a bit. He stood and pulled the horse's head around as he turned back on the trail. He could not clear the trail by himself, and even if he did, by the time the rest of the pack train came up, it would be covered again. Once clear of the drifted trail, he stepped into his saddle and started back to meet the others.

As he approached the others, Old Bill Williams was in the lead with head hunkered down, hat pulled low, chin in his coat and holding the collars of his coat together with a mittened hand, he looked up when his mule stopped. Tate looked at the man and had to holler to make himself heard above the howling wind.

"Can't make it on that trail! We'll have to cut back and move up the lee side of this hill! Only way! Snow's probably fifteen feet deep down in the canyon!"

Williams nodded and motioned for Tate to lead the way. He gigged Shady past the mule and cut across the smooth shoulder of the mountain to find a trail up the lee side, away from the wind. It was a fight all the way, with the first hill no more than three hundred feet to the top. It took almost two hours for the expedition to get everyone the three hundred feet to make it over the top and down into the trees. Several more mules gave out and were left where they lay, but the packs were moved to the stronger animals and they fought their way to keep up.

It was early to make camp, but the next part of the journey would be into the higher mountains and would be even more challenging. Tate had lined out ample camp space for everyone to be in the trees and protected from the wind. He told the men to make bough beds to stay off the ground and try to stay warm. Tired as they were, they knew the young mountain man was right and they took to the trees for the branches needed for their beds.

Tate walked up to the fire where Fremont and others were gathered and saw three men, Dr. Kern one of them, with feet to the fire. One man still had his boots on but the other two had wrestled around to remove their boots and now had stocking feet to the flames. He saw the stockings were frozen stiff and the men were grimacing in pain with frostbitten feet. He watched as Dr. Kern's brother carefully tugged at the socks as they thawed, trying to remove them from his brother's feet. It was a few moments in the doing, but the socks were finally removed to see purplish blue feet. The doctor instructed his brother to begin massaging them to restore the circulation and thaw them out, he spoke through clenched teeth as he struggled to bear the pain.

Tate lifted his eyes and saw the same scene at other fires, men more concerned about frostbitten limbs than getting a warm meal.

It was to be a miserable night for all. Those struggling with frostbite, moaning and crying out, and the others having to listen to the agonies. Then the wind picked up and whistled through the trees, making the pines moan and cry and sound the warning of more misery to come. It was a bedraggled bunch that crawled from their blankets, searching for any warmth from the fires, grasping hot cups of java and sipping the brew to feel it course down their raw throats and settle in their shivering bellies. It seemed that there was no escape from the cold with more fresh snow that came with the wind. The men kept their blankets around them, refusing to leave them to the packs.

Their first attempt to climb the steeper mountain trail was quickly turned back with another wailing wind that blinded the leaders with icy snow. Tate had directed the group, trying to break trail, but the wind had hardened the top crust of the snow and each step broke through and dropped him face down on the icy crust. Shady looked at him with eyes that questioned his sanity and Tate rose from his back and motioned for the men to turn around and go back to camp.

"There ain't no gettin' through that crust!" declared Tate as he stood across the fire from Fremont and Williams. With the wind still howling, he had to holler his words across the fire. "That wind made it thick enough and icy enough to make you think it'll hold ya', but once you step on it, ya break through. And that ice is thick and sharp enough to cut right through ya.'"

"What about takin' one o' these bigger mules? Think they can make it?" asked Williams.

"Won't make it far. That ice'd cut its legs to pieces, an' then you'd have froze mule in your way," answered Tate.

Fremont looked at Tate and Williams, then walked away to another fire. Several men were warming themselves, but Fremont went directly to Charles Taplin who was standing next to Henry King. Both men had been captains in the California Battalion during the third expedition and had proven themselves repeatedly. Fremont said, "Captains Taplin and King, I have a job that I think you men would be especially suited for, as you have done so well before. I need you to get half a dozen other men and take the mauls and beat a path through that crust and snow, so we can make it to the flat top yonder," motioning with a head nod beyond the near mountain. "Now, you might need more men to spell you, but we've got to make it over this mountain. Think you can do it?"

Captain Taplin answered, "We'll do our best, sir." King nodded his head in agreement, both men looking at one another, knowing the job before them would not be an easy one. The men separated and went to the other fires to get their workers and to the packs for the mauls. Tate had followed Fremont and heard his orders to the men. He shook his head as he turned and started back to the trail that he previously started. When the others came alongside, he pointed out the route to take, using the contours of the hillside, and stepped back to watch the men begin their assault. He was surprised as the men began to beat a path through the deep snow and he turned to go back to the camp to have Williams start the train to follow the crew.

"Believe it or not, I think it might work," he said as he stepped to the side of Old Bill. "Those men are breaking that crust and packin' down the loose snow, these mules just might make it. But as sorry as they're lookin', what with no feed an' all, it won't surprise me to see a bunch more of 'em fallin' by the wayside."

"You're shore right 'bout that. Hate to see it, but at least it gives us somethin' to eat," answered the long tall mountain man.

Tate shook his head and started to the trail. He chose to hoof it and lead the Grulla, and when the wind picked up, he was relieved by his choice. Those that rode atop the mules, exposed themselves above the snow and caught the full brunt of the icy wind. With the path cut through the deep snow and the drifts deeper than the height of the elbows on a mounted man, Tate was sheltered from the wind and he and Shady took comfort in one another's nearness.

When he reached the crest of the flat top mountain, he turned to look back at those still struggling up the slope. Several of the riders had realized the advantage of walking and being out of the wind, even though the struggle to make it through the snow was difficult, at least they weren't freezing. But it was another miserable day and difficult climb. Whenever a weak and starving mule fell, the others had to work their way around the downed carcass and move up the trail. Those at the end of the line had a well-broken trail, but had to pass the carcasses of seven mules, some partially butchered for the meat.

15 December, 1848 *The cold and snow are unrelenting and taking a considerable toll on both men and animals. Have lost sixteen mules already and will lose many more. We have no more corn or other feed for the animals and they cannot last. This morning we finally reached the top of the plateau and have seen the lay of the land around. To the north are two higher mountains but the bigger mountains are to our west. Since we are still south of the 38th parallel, we will try for the summit ridge to our northwest. Believe that is the continental divide but won't know until Preuss can take his sightings.*

Made three more miles but lost seven more mules. Trying to keep the packs secure with the many needed items but cannot ask the weary men to carry the heavy loads. We are but a few hundred yards from the summit ridge, but even now the mules are chewing at the blankets, ropes and pads. The extreme weather continues with no let-up. Praying for some break in the wind.

-- John C. Fremont

CHAPTER NINETEEN
SUMMIT RIDGE

"TODAY'S THE DAY WE MAKE THE SUMMIT!" DECLARED Fremont, he turned his back to the fire and pointed to the ridge that held rimrock and stood as a palisade to prevent the expedition from reaching the crest. "If we can make that cut through the rimrock, I believe we can make it to the top, and when we do, we'll cross the continental divide!"

"What's so important about the divide?" asked Godey, standing with arms outstretched to warm his hands by the fire.

"Why, that will mean we have reached the western slope and are over the worst of the mountains!" answered the hopeful Fremont.

Tate looked at Old Bill who stood with head down and shaking, then said, "That ridge don't mean nothin' o' the sort. There's more mountains, and bigger ones, on west of here. You haven't even begun to see the worst of it!"

Fremont looked askance at the young man of the mountains as Tate continued, "And, once you get to the top o' that ridge, you'll find out what cold really is. If you look you can see there ain't no trees or anything else growin' up there."

"Well, isn't that because that's above timberline?"

"Yup, but did you ever wonder why there is a timberline? It's cuz that high up, it's too cold and too windy for anything to grow, 'cept maybe some moss an' tundra an' such. When you get near timberline, the only trees will be windy pines, or some call 'em bristlecones. An' you'll see the branches with the bark turned red from the wind and all the branches growin' on one side, away from the wind. So, even the trees can't hardly stand it."

Fremont stared at Tate, trying to absorb what the man said, and dropped his eyes and rubbed his hands together and with a lower voice added, "Well, we still have to get to the other side, wind or no wind. It's not that far to the crest and we should make it before midday, wouldn't you say, Mr. Williams?"

Old Bill looked at Fremont and drawled, "Oh, we'll make it 'fore noon alright, but it ain't the makin' it that matters, it's gettin' crost' it that counts."

"You too, huh. Well, I'll be right there beside the two of you and we'll just see how bad it is," resolved the leader of the expedition.

Fremont was true to his word and rode side by side with Old Bill and Tate. The men with mauls had preceded them to the rimrock and Tate, now in the lead, pushed Shady through the broken snow searching for the trail that would take them to the top. He looked at the notch between the two escarpments and gigged Shady forward. The wind had been from the west, but Tate noted it had been out of the north, northeast all morning and had turned even colder. The rimrock on either side gave a temporary respite, but the trail was steeper and drifting over. He dropped from the saddle and led the way, trailing Shady right behind him. As he neared the crest, the biting wind tore at his capote, prompting him to grab at the hood and pull it down over his forehead. The sparse bristlecones offered no protection and he fought to push upward.

He stumbled twice, caught himself with his free hand losing the grip on the hood. The wind quickly caught the billowing cowl and exposed his cheeks, but his ears were covered with the fur hat. He ducked his head to the wind and practically crawled over the lip of the crest, facing into the icy blast. He had to lean into the wind and Shady kept tugging at the reins, wanting to be free of the piercing cold. Fremont forced his way to the top, followed by the lanky Williams. The men were leaning into the wind and yet it was pushing them back. Trying to anchor their feet as they leaned, they tried, unsuccessfully, to dig their toes into the frozen tundra. Tate hollered, "Ya see what I mean?"

"Yeah!" answered Fremont as he pointed back to the notch. Tate turned just as Shady jerked the reins as he reared up to turn away from the icy blast. Tate had wrapped the reins around his mittened hand and they had frozen to his palms. When Shady reared, it jerked Tate off his feet and the horse lunged over the edge, pulling Tate behind him. The Grulla was fighting for survival and wanted only to get free of the wind and once over the lip of the precipice, he tried to slide to a stop. The trail from the crest to the notch was too steep for anything but careful footing, and the horse slipped and slid as he twisted and fought for footing. Tate was whipped around and through the drift, taking snow down his neck and in his face. He fought to keep his free hand before his face, and he tumbled over and over and suddenly the rimrock loomed before him. In an instant, he smacked head-first into the abutment and pain and blackness covered him.

MAGGIE STOOD BESIDE SEAN, smiling and with her arms spread wide. Tate walked up the steps, dropped to his knees to hug his son, and stood to embrace his wife. No one spoke, they just looked at one another, touched one another and when Maggie motioned to the open door, Tate led the way into the warm cabin. A fire was crackling in the fireplace, a dutch oven hung from the metal arm and the cabin was filled with the pleasant aroma of good food. He looked in the corner by the bedroom door and saw a Christmas tree. He looked back at Maggie who stood smiling with arms crossed in front of her, and back to the tree. It was decorated with a long string of popcorn, a colorful string of trade beads, simple decorations of painted pine cones and others of bright metal stars. A wispy angel made from scraps of material sat at a slight angle atop the tree. He looked back at his wife and son, held his arms wide and they both came to him.

His forehead felt warm and he lifted his hand and felt something wet, he brought it down and looked to see blood. He looked at Maggie who was still smiling, and back at his hand to the blood. A sharp pain pushed him back and he suddenly felt very cold. He tried to force his eyes open and could only see black, he felt cold and wet and tried again to open his eyes. When he did, a grey blur greeted him and cold pierced him.

"Wal, 'bout time you come to! You ain't gonna let a little bump on the head do you in are ya'?" It was the raspy voice of Old Bill. Tate closed his eyes, felt the searing pain and struggled to open them again. He started to sit up, but his head felt like a cannonball and he couldn't move.

Moving only his eyes, he looked in the direction of the voice and fought to speak, "How long?"

"Oh, less'n an hour. But you took a purty good lick thar, so you just lay thar til you can think straight. You're back at the camp. Fremont finally understood what you was tryin' to tell the stubborn coot and ever'bodys back in camp. We'll try agin' to get o'er that hump or 'round it, anyways."

Old Bill had erected a lean-to of pine boughs that served as a good windbreak for the downed Tate, but the bitter cold still cut through even the best of the coats and blankets. Fremont had given up on taking temperature readings as the knowing of them seemed to make it all the worse. Within the hour, Tate was able to sit up, and he struggled to remove the rest of the snow and ice that had been forced into his capote and even beneath his buckskins. He was better equipped than most with the set of buckskins made by Maggie and lined with rabbit fur. His high-topped moccasins were also fur-lined and with his wool union suit and thick wool woven socks, he had stayed reasonably comfortable, but when the snow and ice penetrated his shell of protection, he shivered with the cold. And once wet, he knew it would be hard to get dry and anything wet would soon turn to ice.

He saw some commotion by the fire at Fremont's camp and asked Bill, "What's goin' on there?" nodding toward the group.

Bill looked toward the group and said, "Don't know. Want me to go find out?"

"Sure, no tellin' what that Fremont'll be wantin' to do. Might pay to know 'bout his plans."

Bill rose and started toward the others as Tate leaned back against the upright of the lean-to but still near the small fire. He pushed a couple of sticks into the flames and lifted his eyes to see Bill returning. As he neared the fire, Tate heard the old man chuckling and saw him shaking his head in amusement.

"You'll never guess what that pilgrim doctor did," he said as he dropped to be seated on a pile of branches. Without waiting for Tate's guess, he added, "That doctor done got his eyes froze shut! Can you imagine? You'd think a doctor'd know better."

"Froze? His eyes?" asked Tate incredulously.

"Yup. An' not only that, when he rode his mule back into camp, he couldn't see where he was goin' an' when the mule stopped he kicked at it. The mule wouldn't go so he kicked it again an' the mule fell over dead! That doctor landed on his face and made it worse! That man can't win fer losin'!"

"How many other mules died?" asked Tate.

"Oh, near's I can tell, we done lost 'bout half of 'em. The rest of 'ems tryin' to eat the blankets, saddle pads, an' each other's mane and tails. Can't blame 'em none. They ain't had nuthin' fer days."

"Yeah, an' I'm gettin' concerned about Shady there. Ain't never seen him lookin' so bad. I'm gonna haf to find some-thin' for him or he won't last much longer," declared Tate, looking over at Shady, tethered in the trees a short distance from the lean-to.

"Yeah, well many more days like today an' these men're gonna start droppin' like them mules. Several more are dealin' with frostbite and this northeast wind is a booger!"

Just the mention of the wind made Tate pull the capote tighter around his middle and reach for his blanket to add to the layers of protection. He scooted a little closer to the flames and watched as Old Bill tried to spear a couple of slices of mule meat to hang over the fire. He knew they were fortunate to have even this meat, but he vowed if they got out of this, he'd never look at the mule the same again. But then he thought about what he just voiced to himself, 'if they got out' and realized this was the first time he dared to consider the possibility they might not make it out of these mountains and Maggie and Sean were waiting. He dropped his head and asked the Lord again, *God, we can't make it without your help. We're gonna need you to show us the way and deliver us from this place.*

IT WAS ONE OF THOSE SPECIAL DAYS WITH BRIGHT WARM SUN, blue sky, and the smell of pine in the air. Maggie pushed with her toe to put the rocker in motion as she sat on the porch watching her son cavort in the clearing with the big wolf. She smiled at the thought of a precocious child of four playing with a massive wolf that had the strength to snap bone with his powerful jaws and even bring down a fleeing elk with his 160 pounds of muscle. And yet her son was sitting astride Lobo who lay on his back letting the boy use his front paws as if they were handles on a cart. The big tongue lolled out of Lobo's mouth and the wolf seemed to be smiling and enjoying the play as much as the boy.

Sean looked up at his mom, "When's Pa comin' home?" He had asked the same question at least once a day for the last two weeks and she always answered, "In a few days. Don't worry, he'll be home before you know it!"

"But when? You said that before, I wan' him home!" and he looked down at Lobo and added, "Lobo does too!"

"I know sweetheart, but your daddy's helping those men and he'll be home just as soon as he can." She stood and walked to the top of the stairs and sat on the top stair, drawing her knees up to rest her chin. "I miss him too. He said he'd do his best to get home by Christmas. I know, how 'bout you and me and Lobo go see if we can find us a Christmas tree?"

The boy jumped up excitedly clapping his hands and ran to the stairs, but Lobo had twisted around and chased after the boy and beat him up the stairs to get some petting from the woman. "Lobo, get back!" declared the child as he pushed at the wolf, wanting to get the same attention from his mother. He lifted his head from her lap and very seriously asked, "Mom, what's a, a Kissmas tree?"

Maggie chuckled at her son's expression and sat him down beside her as she began to explain, "Well, every year at about this time, people all over the world take a day to honor the birth of Jesus Christ, our Saviour, and that day is called Christmas."

"I know Jesus, but why a tree?"

"Well that's a little harder to understand. But the reason we do a tree, is because it is an evergreen, you know," as she pointed to the many pines around the clearing, "because it is always green, even in the winter. What that says is it tells us about eternal life, how when we have Jesus as our Savior, we have eternal life, like the evergreen. Even after the tree is cut down and taken into the house, it is still green to show that life. And we decorate it as we show our happiness about the life Jesus gives us. And we give gifts to remind us of the gift of eternal life that Jesus paid for when he died on the cross."

"Ummm, that's good." He jumped up and said, "Let's go get a tree!"

Maggie smiled at her son, knowing he probably didn't fully understand what she tried to explain, but knowing her curious boy, she knew he would think about it and ask questions until he could understand. She was pleased that he was one who never let anything go until he was satisfied and he knew all he wanted to know about whatever had piqued his curiosity. She dropped her head as she remembered her own childhood and the many times her mother, exasperated at some of her questions, would say, "Go ask your father!" She smiled as she thought there would be plenty of times when she would probably send her children to their father for their answers to many of life's questions. And she chuckled to herself as she thought that she had just said to herself, 'children'.

She struggled to get Sean to hold still as she bundled him up for the cold. She had made matching outfits of fur-lined buckskins for her two men and a similar one for herself and she held tightly to the small jacket as she pulled it together to be fastened with the antler buttons and loops. It was warm enough outside that the buckskins would be adequate, and they weren't going far, as she had already picked out just the right tree for their holiday.

With the Hawken slung across her back, the Paterson in her belt holster, and the metal blade tomahawk tucked in her belt, she took Sean's hand in hers and they started to the woods. With a wave of her hand, Lobo trotted off before them, bounding through the fluffy snow that covered the trail. It was just a short while before they came to the bend in the trail that marked the spot where Maggie had seen the tree, and they turned into the woods, wading through the snow that was just over ankle deep on the woman.

"There it is!" exclaimed Maggie, pointing out the tree to Sean. The boy jerked his hand from his mothers and started jumping through the snow that came almost to his knees, heading for the designated tree. He fell forward into the snow, laughing, and rolled to his back to sit up and look at his mother. Maggie laughed with the boy, and asked, "Can you get up alright?"

"Ummhummm, watch!" he declared as he pushed himself to his feet and stood up proudly. Maggie started for the tree and Sean stumbled after. She walked around the blue spruce, checking for broken branches as she shook each one to free it from the snow. Sean grabbed a couple of the lower branches and shook them, but the snow from the upper branches shook loose and tumbled in his face, making him lift his hands to wipe his face as he stumbled backwards and fell again, only this time he was sitting and looking up at the rebellious tree.

Maggie looked at the bewildered expression on her son and smiled, "What's the matter? Get a little snow on you?"

He rolled over to put out his hands and push himself up and brushed himself off as he stepped back away from the tree. "Yeah!" he declared as he considered leaving the tree cutting to his mother. Besides, it was more fun to just play in the snow while she did the work. He turned and looked around for Lobo.

Maggie tramped the snow down around the base of the tree and stood back to decide just where she would start cutting. As she looked, she began taking the Hawken from her back and thought she would need to prop it against the trunk of a nearby towering spruce, so she would be free to chop down their Christmas tree. With the Hawken in hand she turned away from their chosen tree and froze in her tracks. Sean had fallen face down in the snow and was flouncing around as he fought to get up, but less than ten feet from her son, the biggest lynx she had ever seen was watching the boy, one foot lifted and looking ready to pounce. Without thinking of anything but her boy, Maggie brought the Hawken to her shoulder, cocking the hammer and setting the triggers as she did, thinking, *I did put a cap on the nipple, didn't I?*

The lynx shifted his weight to his big back legs, readying

his pounce, and just as he started to spring, Maggie fired the Hawken with an explosion that caused several of the branches to loose the new fallen snow tumbling to the ground. She dropped the butt of the Hawken to the ground, trying to see through the cloud of grey smoke that belched from the rifle. She saw a shocked Sean turn to look at his mother, and then was surprised to see Lobo standing astraddle of the downed Lynx, growling with teeth bared and eyes slit, ready for any move of the feline.

Maggie quickly reloaded the rifle, strictly by feel, afraid to take her eyes off the lynx and her son. She called to Sean, "Come here!" as she put the cap on the nipple and brought the hammer to full cock to set the triggers. She pointed to the ground beside her and said, "Stay here!" as she began to walk slowly toward the wolf and lynx. "Lobo, here!" motioning to her side. The wolf snarled one more time at the still form of the lynx and trotted to the side of Maggie. She looked at the crumpled form of mottled grey fur, moved closer, reached out with the muzzle of the rifle to poke it, and satisfied, let out the breath she had been holding and stood, relaxing. She looked down at Lobo, "Good boy, good boy," and back at Sean, "You can come here now."

As they examined the carcass, Maggie saw the lynx had one bad eye, apparently injured in some kind of fight, and an injured leg. With the injuries, she believed the cat had resorted to going after anything for food, even that which would not normally be considered his prey. She thought to herself that she had never considered herself or her child to be prey, but that was apparently what the lynx saw when the boy was struggling in the snow. She pulled Sean close beside her and mumbled a simple prayer, *Thanks Lord. If you hadn't made me see it in time, my boy could have been lost. Thank you.*

Maggie stood looking down at the carcass, then back to the tree, and said to Sean, "Well, looks like we got a little more work to do, so, you stay close now." Then looking at Lobo, "You stay close too."

She chose to use only the pelt from the lynx and pulled the carcass to the rockpile to let Lobo do with it as he willed, but she was surprised to see Lobo totally ignore the carcass, choosing instead to romp with the boy. She cut down the tree, lay the pelt across the branches, and tying a long rawhide thong to the trunk, she let Sean help her drag the tree back to the house. As they struggled up the stairs, she thought about what she would use to decorate the tree and how she would make a stand for it. But for now, with the tree on the porch, she leaned the Hawken against the wall and plopped down in the rocker for a much-deserved rest. Sean crawled up in her lap and within a short while, mother, son, and wolf were all asleep as the afternoon sun bent its rays through the tall pines to warm the figures at the cabin. A slow smile crept across Maggie's face as she dreamed of the soon return of her mountain man.

CHAPTER TWENTY-ONE
DESOLATION

TATE WAS NOW FORCED TO TAKE HIS DAILY ALONE TIME WITH his God while wrapped in his blankets and huddled under the edge of the lean-to. The storm continued unabated and he peeked out from the edge of the pine boughs to search the sky for any blue but was again disappointed. He shook his head as he struggled to read from the book of Proverbs and he strained to see one of his favorite passages, but it almost hurt to read it, *Trust in the Lord with all thine heart; and lean not unto thine own understanding. In all thy ways acknowledge him, and he shall direct thy paths.* He lifted his eyes heavenward as he prayed, *But God, that's what I've been doing! And I'm waitin' for you to show me the right path!* He looked back at the scripture and continued to read, *Be not wise in thine own eyes* . . . He shook his head in wonder and added to his prayer, *Alright, whatever you say.* He pushed his Bible back into the saddle bags he had used for a pillow, scooted forward and stood, dropping his blanket and walked to the fire.

Bill Williams looked up as Tate approached, "Wal, you ain't lookin' much better, but I've seen worse! You look like you got sumpin' on yore mind, let's have at it. You got some idee that'll git us outta this mess?"

Tate stood before the fire, hands outstretched as he looked around at the expectant faces of Williams, Godey, and Josiah Ferguson. The three experienced frontiersmen had been talking with one another for some time and Tate could tell by their empty expressions, that none had given any promise of hope. He started, "Well, yeah, I've been thinkin' just like all you have. And the way I see it is we ain't got any more chance o' gettin' through them mountains than a scared rabbit has in a hungry wolf's den." The others nodded their heads in agreement, but still looked expectantly to the youngest of the group. "I don't know how long it's gonna take for that mule-headed Fremont to come to that same conclusion, but I'm thinkin' 'bout findin' a way outta here, you know, a way to get back down to the Rio Grande and on outta here, instead o' tryin' to do the impossible tryin' to get through these mountains in this snowstorm."

"Wal, just what'chu thinkin', young'un?" drawled Bill, voicing what the three had been thinking and discussing.

"I'm thinkin' if'n I head off thataway," pointing to the southeast, "I b'lieve there's a way back o'er the hump and down into Embargo Creek. If'n we can make that, then it'll be easier goin' to follow the creek down to the Rio Grande. 'Course there ain't gonna be no easy way outta this mess, but that might be the best way."

"Cain't be no worse'n this! Most o' the fellers are already callin' this Camp Desolation!" declared Ferguson.

The others nodded, and Old Bill said, "Ain't that the truth. Ain't seen so much desolation in the eyes of men than this bunch."

"Can't blame 'em! We been fightin' this durn snow fer o'er a week now, an' it's snowed more'n three feet, an' we ain't made more miles'n what we coulda made in one day, if'n we had decent weather!" proclaimed Ferguson. The small group had been joined by Henry Wise and Thomas Breckenridge, both experienced frontiersmen from Missouri that joined Ferguson on the third expedition.

"Yup, an' I thought Fremont was stubborn when we was in Californy, but this hyar snowstorm's done froze his stubbornness ever harder!" proclaimed Breckenridge.

"Well, fellas, it'll prob'ly take me a couple days to find us a way through, but I'll be back. In the meantime, be careful with them fireholes. You keep puttin' your blankets down next to them fires, and with the fire meltin' it's way down, you're liable to end up buried!" explained Tate.

The men chuckled, knowing what he said was true. With the party broken up into messes, or groups that ate together, the fires they made would naturally melt the surrounding snow, and by the time to turn in for the night, the fire had melted it's way deep enough so that the surrounding hole and fire were too deep to be seen by nearby mess groups. But the hole protected them from the wind and the remaining fire provided enough warmth to get some sleep. However, all too often the sleepers would awaken to as much as three or four feet of fresh snow and caved in walls almost burying them. But good judgment had been dispelled by the miserable cold and the men found themselves doing anything to get relief from the bitterness of winter.

When Tate finished gearing up Shady, he walked to the fire and drew Old Bill aside, "Now Bill, you know what I said is true, and these men ain't used to these altitudes and thin air and they don't think straight. That's why I'm thinkin' we need to get 'em outta these mountains. We get back down to the river, get some fresh venison, mebbe get warmed up a mite, they should be alright. Don'tchu think?"

"You know, I plumb forgot 'bout how this altitude affects them flatlanders! You're right, it ain't just the cold an' hunger that's makin' 'em think strange." He was shaking his head as he spoke, remembering his own bouts with altitude sickness. He looked at Tate and instructed, "You be careful now, y'hear? You find us a good route outta here an' get back. We're countin' on you."

Tate stepped aboard his GrullaGrulla and started for the cut in the trees that would take him onto the open south-facing slope. Tate had scouted his route with his scope from within the cover of the trees, but that had not shown the depth of the snow. But worse than the depth, which he calculated to be not much more than a foot, was the hard crust fashioned by sun melting just enough of the surface snow to be frozen by the constantly blowing wind. Every step made by Shady would require a forcible breaking of the crust before pushing forward to make another difficult step. They were less than halfway across the open slope when Shady stopped, breathing heavily, and refusing to move any further. Tate slipped from the saddle, grabbed the spade he had taken from the camp for this very purpose, and started breaking the trail for the two of them. He would cut through the crust, shovel away some of the underlying pieces and a couple spades full of loose snow, then repeat.

By the time they crossed the open slope and found the shelter of the timber, it was well past mid-day. Tate found a sizable rock, kicked the snow from enough space for him to sit and rest and started munching on the last of the pemmican in his pack. Shady sniffed at his hands, looking for something to eat, but Tate put the last bit in his mouth and showed empty hands to the hungry horse. He reached out and stroked the Grulla's face and said, "I'll get you somethin' soon, boy, I promise." With that he slid from the rock and mounted up to find the expected return route to the river.

With the trees holding much of the snow and protecting the trail from the winds, it was a little easier going through the black timber. Although the snow was still well over two feet deep and in places the natural drifts over four feet deep, he was able to work his way in the general direction he had planned. After over an hour, the near hillside grew considerably steeper and showing sheer cliffs. He leaned forward and tried to see through the thick trees, then gigged Shady from the trail and into the thicker trees. He stepped down and slipped a rein over a branch and forced his way through the close-growing grove of naked aspen. What he thought he had seen showed itself as a black scar on the face of the grey cliff face. Whether just an overhang or cave he didn't know but was determined to find out as he pushed his way through the interlaced and snow-laden branches. Soon he stood at the opening and could see it was at least enough of an overhang for protection for both him and his horse. He looked back through the trees to where Shady stood and knew this was the answer he had been looking for and for which he prayed. He saw what would pass for a trail through the trees that would be easier going for Shady and started stomping snow as he returned for his horse.

As he moved through the aspen, he glanced to the creek bottom no more than forty yards away. He stopped and looked. What he saw were the bent over branches of heavy laden willows, forming mounds and mounds of snow on both sides of an iced-over creek. This was near the headwaters of Wannamaker creek and the wind had kept the snow in the creek bottom from piling as deep as in the lower ranges. He let a slow smile cross his face as he remembered the way the willow covered creek banks looked in the summer months. He looked to Shady and said, "You're gonna like this!"

They stopped back away from the willows, and Tate stepped down, spade in hand. He slapped at the bent over willows with the spade, sending snow flying in all directions

and making Shady toss his head as he backed away. Tate
continued his onslaught and turned his attention to the loose
snow that fell from the now upright willows and feverishly
shoveled it aside. After several minutes of laborious work, he
stood up straight with one hand at his now sore back and
looked back at Shady and said, "Well, c'mon. I thought you
were hungry!" and motioned to the uncovered thick grass
that lay sheltered under the overhanging willows. Shady
quickly stepped to the cleared area and wasted no time crop-
ping the tasty, though faded brown, grass. Tate stuck the
spade in the drift and plopped down on the pile of snow,
content to watch his horse take his fill.

Once he caught his breath, Tate sat up and looked
around. Although it was still overcast, at least it wasn't
snowing and blowing, and he had a pretty good view of his
anticipated route. As he traced his probable route with his
slow gaze, a movement nearby caught his eye and he slowly
turned his head to see a big jackrabbit standing on his over-
sized snowshoe hind feet, ears erect as he watched this
mousy colored horse invading his domain. Tate carefully
slipped his Paterson from the holster and brought it to bear
on the white-furred rabbit. He squeezed off a shot that startled Shady, but only enough for him to lift his head and see
what Tate was doing before returning to his feast. The
jackrabbit flipped end over end at the impact of the bullet
and Tate jumped up to retrieve his supper.

CHAPTER TWENTY-TWO
DECISION

21 DECEMBER, 1848 *IT HAS BEEN A MISERABLE THREE DAYS. Temperature stays at about 20º below zero, and wind seldom slacks. We have tried for these three days to push forward, but when we cut a trail through the snow that has drifted as high as fifteen feet, with pots and dinner plates, by the time we can load the few remaining mules and attempt the passage, the wind has covered it over as if we were never there. Three messes of men, all struggling. Have lost most of the mules to cold and starvation. Difficult to see the valiant animals with ears frozen and legs cracked and bleeding from the cold. Thought we saw grass yesterday but only the tops of brush and of no benefit. Nights are so cold we often wake with whiskers, hair, clothing, bedding all frozen together. Scraped a foot of snow from bedrolls but by the time we turned in, another foot had fallen. We are of all men most miserable. Fear we must quit and try to return to the river before men start falling as the mules have. If we do not have fair weather on the morrow, will decide about quitting.*

--John C. Fremont

"Hey Old Bill! The colonel wants to see you. Is that young'un back yet?" shouted Alexis Godey, seeking to be heard over the whistling wind.

"If you mean Tate, no, ain't seen hide nor hair of him. Was hopin' you was him when I heerd you hollerin'!" answered the long tall frontiersman.

"Wal, you need to go see what he's a wantin' anyhow."

Bill nodded his head as he turned to lean into the unrelenting wind. He ducked his head to take the force of the icy blast and trudged forward to make his way to Fremont's camp. The tent only stood partially erect and served only as a windbreak against the onslaught of old man winter. Fremont and two others sat between the canvas barrier and the flickering flames. Bill dropped down beside the trio and shivered to shake the fresh snow from his capote. The howling gale was not as loud here, but he still had to speak loudly, "You wanted to see me?"

"Do you think we can make it over that hump and any further?" asked a hopeful but realistic Fremont.

"Colonel, you keep tryin' what'chu been doin' the last three days and the only thing that'll get'chu is a big pile o' dead bodies! These men are fadin' fast and the mules'll all be gone in a couple more days. An' with the mules gone, these men can't pack nuthin' and there won't even be mule meat for eatin'!" declared an exasperated Williams. "An' you fer durn sure ain't gonna get no railroad o'er these mountains, leastways not in the winter!"

"Where's Tate?" asked Fremont.

"He left a couple days ago, should be back anytime. He went lookin' for a way back outta here, one these worn out men an' mules might be able to make."

"But we hadn't decided to turn back!" proclaimed an angered Fremont.

"Nope, but we figgered you'd come to yore senses soon 'nuff, and he wanted to have a way fer us to go."

Fremont's shoulders slumped as he realized the high price of his stubbornness and knew he should be grateful for the foresight of Saint, but he was used to unwavering loyalty and obedience and anything less smacked of rebellion. He shook his head at the thought and reminded himself that the foresight of the young man just might save some lives. He looked up at Williams, "Alright, let me know when he gets back. In the meantime, let the men know we'll be turning back and they can start getting ready."

WITH FULL BELLIES and a warm night, both Tate and Shady were feeling stronger when they broke the trail to the crest of the saddle on the ridge. With a full day to make it to the top and over to the trees beyond, Tate recognized the watershed as the headwaters of Embargo Creek. He had hunted for elk in this very area just last fall and he knew this would be their way back to the Rio Grande. He returned to the Wannamaker creek and cleared more snow from the willows for Shady to once again eat his fill before they returned to the previous night's shelter in the cavern.

It was early morning and the grey band of first light was just beginning to make shadows of the eastern mountains when Tate was awakened by a ruckus outside and below the cavern. He looked to see Shady facing the opening with ears forward and nostrils flared. Tate grabbed his Hawken, checked the load and cap, slipped the Paterson into the holster and strode to the cavern mouth to discern the noise. He could only see vague forms in the darkness, silhouetted against the white snow, but the sounds told him a pack of wolves had taken down some game.

He moved warily through the aspen, carefully choosing

his steps in the soft snow. As he neared the edge of the trees, he could make out at least three wolves that appeared to be tearing at the carcass of an elk. This was meat that he and the men could use. He lifted the Hawken as he eared back the hammer, setting the triggers. In one smooth but slow motion, he brought the front blade sight down on the largest of the wolves and when it lined up with the buckhorn sight at the back, he squeezed the front trigger. The explosion rocked the stillness of the mountains and the Hawken spit fire as it sent the ball hurtling to take down the big wolf.

Tate quickly lowered the rifle, keeping his eyes on the melee at the elk's carcass. The big wolf had been sent tumbling beyond the carcass and the other two had frozen, turning only their heads as the orange of their eyes gleamed from their dark silhouettes, searching for their attacker. Tate slipped the Paterson from the holster and brought it to bear on the second wolf, but as he squeezed off his shot, both wolves started their quick retreat. He only wounded the one that whimpered and tucked its tail as it slunk off after the other.

Tate waited a few moments, loading the Hawken before he left his cover. Then with no sign of the wolves, he walked to the carcass. The elk had been ripped and chewed, but he found the two quarters on the underneath side would be usable, as well as the backstraps. He made short work of the butchering and with the Hawken slung over his back, he dragged the two quarters behind him as he struggled back up the slope to the cavern. Under other circumstances, he would have taken the time to salvage the hide of the elk and the pelt of the wolf, but those things were not important now, just the meat.

Once back inside the cavern and with the sun bending its rays through the aspen, Tate rekindled his fire and began preparing his breakfast of choice slices of backstrap. He drooled at the thought but bided his time with a cup of fresh coffee as he watched the steaks broiling and dripping their juices into the flames. He munched on a handful of rose hips and kinnikinnick while he waited.

He knew the men would be hungry for something besides mule meat so he de-boned the hind quarter and packed the partial backstrap and the meat together, lashing it behind the cantle of the saddle. He put the front quarter and the other backstrap on a bed of branches on a high up ledge in the cavern, planning on retrieving it when the expedition retraced his recently found route over the ridge. Once again with full stomachs and a good night's warm rest, he and Shady started back to the camp of the expedition.

It was a miserable looking bunch that peered from under their scarfs, capote hoods, and floppy hats held down with long straps or scarfs. The wind had subsided a little, but it was still biting as Tate rode into the camp. He slipped from the saddle, grinning at the forlorn faces, and removed the elk meat, and handed it to a bug-eyed Williams, "Brought you some elk steaks, think you could use it?"

"Use it? If it weren't froze I'd be chewin' on it already!" he declared as he turned to Breckenridge, "I reckon we oughta share it with the colonel, so cut him off a chunk 'fore I put it on the fire!" He turned back to Tate, "So, did'ju find us a way outta here?"

"Yup, sure did. Done been o'er it and back again. That'll take us out at the headwaters of Embargo Creek!"

"Why, if'n we can get there, it'll be just a hop, skip an' a jump on down to the Rio Grande!" answered a hopeful Williams. "Why, if these ol' bones weren't so froze up, I'd be dancin' a jig!" He laughed as he slapped his leg and added, "By jove, that'll give these fellers some hope. Maybe even get o'er that ridge in time for Christmas! An' if'n there's more elk where this came from, why, we might even have a good

Christmas dinner, yessir!" He looked at Tate again, "An' if'n we make it, since they been callin' this Camp Desolation, I'm gonna call that new place Camp Hope!" he declared, nodding his head and grinning as he lay the backstrap on the rocks beside the fire, licking his lips in anticipation. "Yessir, that's what I'm gonna do!"

CHAPTER TWENTY-THREE
HOPE

WHEN TATE ROLLED FROM HIS BLANKETS, HE WAS SURPRISED to see the camp already abuzz with activity. The men had heard the good news that they were headed back down and were reinvigorated with the hope and the real possibility of survival. Tate knew from the fireside conversations that most had resigned themselves to a fate of starvation or freezing. His news of a passable route and the possibility of fresh meat had done as much as a warm meal to give the men a boost of morale. He walked to the fire, now protected by a lean-to, and looked to Old Bill who was standing with a wide grin as he watched the younger man approach.

"Wal, 'bout time you got up! Why, 'fore ya' know it the sun'll be shinin' an' the camp'll be movin'! Course, we sorta need you to show us the way, but I figger we'll make out. But, how 'bout you startin' ahead with the crew and the mauls and such so y'all can make a trail fer us muleskinners?"

"Can't I even get sumpin' to eat 'fore I head out?" asked a still sleepy Tate.

"Ain't got nuthin'! But you can have a cup o' weak coffee.

That's the last o' the Arbuckles," he said, nodding to the steaming coffee pot.

Tate poured himself a cup of the steaming brew, noting its pale color, but sipped at it anyway. He noticed several men struggling with the lean and stubborn mules, trying to get the packs loaded and ready to move. As he watched, a group of men carrying mauls and pots walked to the fire and looked to Tate. One man spoke, "We been told to get a move on. You ready?"

Tate nodded his head, chugged the last of the weak coffee, and answered, "Let me get my horse an' I'll be right with you."

By the time Tate and the maul crew reached the aspen grove near the cavern, the sun was well up and doing its best to penetrate the thick cloud cover with a little bit of encouraging sunshine. Standing just inside the tree line, Tate pointed out the trail to the crew, "You can still make out where I broke trail yesterday. You can see it makes for the near side of that saddle. Watch your footin' when you cross the creek yonder, it's not too deep there, but that north facing slope is deceiving. It gets purty deep up there, but the crust ain't too bad."

The man that seemed to be the ramrod of the crew, Charles Taplin, nodded his head and started from the trees. The rest of his crew followed, and everyone started swinging the big-headed mauls, widening the narrow trail cut by Tate. The crew of eight was to be relieved at midday and they in turn would take over handling the mules. Tate watched the men, tired, cold, hungry and desperate, fight against the cold. The wind had started in again and the shoveled snow, stacked on the downwind side, would soon be scattered as if it was never there. Fortunately, the snow from the night before had been a heavy wet snow and the wind quickly turned it into a thick crust. The crust made it harder to break the trail, but it kept the wind from filling in their work with blown snow.

Tate went to the cavern and started a fire. This place could be used for the relief of workers, giving them a break from the wind and cold. He cut several small branches from the aspen and sliced the backstrap. He hung the slices over the fire and sat back to enjoy the warmth. It was just a short while when Tate heard the noises of the rest of the expedition following their trail and he stepped to the cavern mouth to watch. He saw Old Bill and he hollered out, "Hey old man! Come on up and warm yourself!"

Williams looked up to see his friend standing out of the wind and smiling down at him. He motioned to those nearby and these few leaders, well distanced from the others, started through the aspen to the cavern. He stomped his feet as he stepped under the overhang and looked to Tate, "Is that meat I smell cookin'?"

"It is, but I'm savin' most of it for them trail breakers up there. When they get relieved, I figger they're gonna need it worse'n anybody else. But, I reckon there might be a couple slices to spare."

Williams, Breckenridge, Godey, and Josiah Ferguson walked to the fire and gratefully accepted a slice of broiled elk backstrap and wasted little time devouring the morsel. They looked hungrily at the rest of the slices dripping their juices on the flames, but Tate reminded them, "We need to save that for them trail breakers. They're gonna need it."

The others lifted their eyes to Tate and nodded their heads in agreement. Each man knew without the trailbreakers, no one would be going anywhere, and everyone wanted away from this place. Williams said, "Wal, what we had was more'n we expected, and this hyar fire shore feels mighty fine. Say, Ferguson, how 'bout you checkin' to see if'n them fellers have reached the top yet?" The younger man, one of the Missouri frontiersman, nodded his head and flipped the hood up on his capote as he walked from the cavern.

"Just how far is it o'er that saddle, anyway?" asked Williams looking at Tate.

"From here to where we'll prob'ly camp, not more'n two miles. But gettin' this bunch and all them packs over there's gonna take a couple days at least. Snow's worst on this side, but th'other side's purty deep too. When I went over there, I stopped 'fore I got into the deep stuff an' I was armpit deep as it was," explained Tate. "So, down closer to them trees, I reckon it'll be, oh, ten to fifteen feet deep. But the way them boys is doin', they'll prob'ly make a purty good trench to make it through."

Ferguson walked into the opening of the cavern and said, "The first crew's comin' down. Ya want me to tell 'em to come in here?"

Tate answered, "Yeah, tell we got some food for 'em. That'll get 'em in here sure 'nuff."

The others chuckled at his remark, knowing he could probably start a stampede of hungry men by mentioning warm food. In a short while, the crew of eight maulers were stomping their feet under the overhang and looking into the darker cavern. The only light had been from the fire and that coming in the opening, but the crowd at the entry made the cavern darker. The smell of cooking meat brought the men hustling in, eyes wide as they saw the meat hanging over the fire, dripping its juices into the snapping flames. Tate did the honors and handed each man a stick with a sizzling slice of backstrap and watched as each was eagerly devoured.

"Did you make it to the crest of that saddle?" asked Tate of Taplin.

"Not quite, but it shouldn't take long to get there. We were gettin' close when we were relieved," answered the leader of the crew.

Tate looked to Williams and suggested, "Maybe if you pick out another crew, give 'em some meat 'fore they go, they might make it down th' other side, an' we can have camp there tonight."

24 DECEMBER, 1848 *Three days have been spent moving the packs and baggage to the new camp. The men worked beyond expectation, digging the trail through the snow. We now have a trench, deeper than the tallest man, to ferry our gear over the mountain. At least the wind has abated somewhat but our supplies have dwindled to a single bag of macaroni, one of rice and two small bags of sugar. Godey has promised a good meal for tomorrow, Christmas day, but I don't see how he can manage. We had to dig out our camp with dinner plates and pots and have cleared down six feet to make as good a camp as possible. Must rest here before continuing. We are hopeful of finding game but have seen no sign. I am considering sending a party of experienced men to try to reach a settlement and find help. If they can make it, we stand a chance of survival. I am fearful of our chances with no supplies. Lost more mules and I believe we will have to kill the others for their meat. What to do with the baggage? Still more on the other side, some stacked on top of the crossing. The men know it is just equipment and other gear and are loathe to move the heavy parcels. Will probably be forced to leave much behind. Tate Saint did bring in some elk meat and the men are calling the new camp, Camp Hope. Perhaps there is hope after all.*

- John C. Fremont

CHAPTER TWENTY-FOUR
CHRISTMAS

CHRISTMAS DAWNED BRIGHT WITH SOME BLUE SKY AND JUST A touch of sunshine. Tate and Shady shared their cavern with Old Bill and Breckenridge, and the three stirred from their blankets to greet the first sight of sunshine and blue sky since before they left the Rio Grande more than two weeks earlier. Tate looked at the others as he pushed the coffee pot nearer the fire. This was the last of his own spare rations of coffee, but he felt obligated to share with the others. As they sat watching the shaking of the pot as it perked the coffee, the smell filled the cavern and slow smiles began to paint the somber faces. Tate was the first to speak, "Hey, I just remembered, it's Christmas!"

Old Bill looked at his young friend and drawled, "So, what'd you get me for Christmas?"

"You're lookin' at it," answered Tate as he nodded toward the coffee pot. "An' that's more'n most are gettin' today!"

Breckenridge grunted, "Ain't that the goshawful truth! Never thot I'd be spendin' Christmas in a cave in a mountain with the likes o' you two surrounded by this much snow!" He stared into the flames as he let his mind loose to travel the halls of memory and Christmases past.

"Wal, we better get a move on and get o'er to the new camp. Godey's s'posed to fix us a big meal for the holiday, an' I don' wanna miss it," stated Old Bill, also staring into the flames. The thought of the special day and the many memories that accompanied the remembrance filled the men with melancholy as their eyes took on the glazed over appearance of one whose thoughts were elsewhere.

Tate stood and stretched, walked back to the high ledge and pulled down the reserved front quarter of elk. He walked back to the fire with the leg bone over his shoulder and said, "We don't hafta worry 'bout missin' dinner," and grinned as the men looked up with eyes wide.

"Why you young whippersnapper you!" declared Old Bill as he stood and looked at the burden on Tate's shoulder. "We better get a move on, or Godey'll make sign stew an' pine puddin' and call it good. But with this, why, them fellers'll think they done died an' gone ta' Heaven!"

Most of an hour passed before the three men made it into the new camp. There was little activity save for a few gathered at a couple of fires. When Tate led Shady to the camp of Fremont and Godey, he was greeted with little more than grunts and nods. But when he dropped the elk quarter at the feet of Godey, everyone came awake and started shouting as if they were in a camp meeting in the woods. Fremont said, "That's gotta be the best Christmas present ever! By gum, we need ta' be giving thanks for that. If God ever answered prayer, He sure done it this time!" He looked at a grinning Tate and then to Old Bill, "Bill, I know you done a bit a preaching in your day. You were a Protestant preacher, weren't you?"

"Yeah, but most of my time was spent with the Osage Indians as a missionary of sorts," explained Williams.

"How 'bout giving us a Christmas message this morning? I think the men'd appreciate some encouragement from the Scriptures, don't you?"

"I s'pose I can do that. Gimme a bit an' I'll get muh Bible and when the men all get together, make sure there's a nice warm fire, then I'll say a word or two," answered Bill, turning away to retrieve his Bible from his packs. It was just a short while before the rest of the men had gathered around the now stoked up fire of Fremont. With logs, rocks, and packs for seats, the men looked expectantly at Old Bill as he stood before them, Bible in hand. He bowed his head and closed his eyes and muttered a silent prayer for a helping hand from the Lord and lifted his eyes to the men.

"As you fellers know, this is Christmas day. An' I know that you've prob'ly all heard what most call the Christmas story. You know, 'bout how Joseph and Mary went to Nazareth and she was with child and gave birth to Jesus. That's what we usually talk about on Christmas day."

Tate was listening, and watching the men and noticed Old Bill began talking without his usual drawl of mountain man vernacular, but more as the educated man he was, much like so many of the men in the mountains. Tate grinned as he thought about how so many came from fine families with a background of higher education and great experience, but when they came to the mountains, they became so much like other men in the wilderness, leaving the past behind. Tate listened closely as Bill continued.

"Here in the book of Luke, second chapter, is the account of the angel appearing to Mary and Joseph and sayin', *For unto you is born this day in the city of David, a Saviour, which is Christ the Lord.* Now what I want you to think about is those two words, *a Saviour.* Now, we are in a pretty tight spot up here in these mountains and all this snow. And it might be we don't get out of it. So, here's what we need to think about, whether we get out or not, is do you know Christ the Lord as your Savior? No, I don't mean do you know about Jesus. It's not what you know about, it's do you know Him as your Savior.

"You see fellas, we're all alone up here on this mountain and it would be good if we had somebody come and save us, you know, get us down from here and back home safe and sound. That's one way of bein' saved, isn't it?" He looked around at the uplifted expectant faces and saw several nodding and even looking to one another. "Yeah, it is. But the way things are now, it doesn't look like anybody's coming to save us. So, what if we don't get out of these mountains, then what?" Again, he looked from one man to the other, saw everyone sitting stone still and continued, "If we ended up spending the last days of our lives right here on this mountain, and died, then what? You see, fellas, the time will come, whether soon or not, that we will have to face our eternity. And the Bible tells us there's only one way to get to Heaven, and that way is Jesus."

He paused and flipped a few pages in his Bible and resumed, "You see the Bible says right here in John 14:6 *I am the way, the truth, and the life. No man cometh unto the Father but by me.* See, when He said *by me* that's it. You see, too many think they're goin' to Heaven because they've been good people, or maybe it's because they believe in God, or because they're members of a church. But it's none of that. When He says *by me* He's telling us He is the only way, not one way, but the only way. He alone can be our Savior and He becomes our Savior in only one way, and that's by taking that step and putting our trust totally in Him. That's when we trust only Him to save us, to take us to Heaven when we die.

"So, I'm here to tell you fellas, if you haven't done it before, you need to do it now. If you want to make Heaven your home, and I don't mean go to Heaven today but just shall we say, get your ticket, then here's what you need to do. Just ask Jesus to be your Savior, and you gotta mean it with all your heart. Just say a simple prayer, between you and God, and ask Him to forgive your sins and come into your life and be your Savior and take you to Heaven when you die. It's that simple, don't you think you ought to do that on this Christmas day?" He looked at all the men, many nodding their heads. "Then, just bow your head and say your own prayer, get things settled today."

He paused, saw several heads bowed and waited for them to lift, then said, "Alright, now I'm gonna pray an' ask the Lord to bless the fine dinner that ol' Godey there's a fixin' for us." He bowed his head and prayed aloud, asking God to bless the men that prayed to receive Christ as their Savior, and asking God to bless the meal they were about to share. He added, "And God, it sure would be mighty fine if you get us outta these mountains. Don't know how you're gonna do it, but we're sure askin' for your help. In Jesus name, Amen!" The crowd of men echoed the amen so loudly some of the snow still clinging to the pine boughs tumbled and dropped in piles below. The crowd laughed and began talking with one another, showing the best spirit seen for many days.

And it was a fine meal with elk stew, rice doughnuts, biscuits, and mule meat pie. Godey had stashed away some coffee and proudly presented a large pot of hot black java to top off the best meal the men had in almost two weeks. Although it didn't make the men forget their perilous situation, it did take it from their minds for a little while, and that was a special blessing indeed.

CHAPTER TWENTY-FIVE
RELIEF

"BILL, I WANT YOU TO TAKE THREE MEN, BRECKENRIDGE, Henry King, and Creutzfeldt there," motioning to the last of the three standing beside the fire. "And I want you fellas to go for relief. We're not going to make it without some help and you four can travel a lot farther and faster than the entire crew."

Old Bill Williams looked at Fremont and could tell this decision had been hard on the stubborn leader of the men. He had known that hard decisions made as a leader were difficult at best, but when mixed with the stubborn determination of a man like Fremont, any decision that included the failure of a mission, would be doubly hard. Bill watched the muscles of Fremont's jaw work as he gritted his teeth, not against the cold, but against what had to be done. Bill dropped his eyes as Fremont continued.

"You know this country best of these men, so Bill I'm thinking you can make it to Socorro or Taos and find supplies and mules and get some more men to return and give aid. I'm going to split the group and we will follow, but as you know, we won't be able to make the time and distance of your group."

"What about supplies? And mules?" asked Bill.

"We'll give you all we can spare, which is mighty little. There's a bait of sugar, some macaroni, and some tallow candles, but can't let you have any mules. I know we're asking a lot of you men," he looked from one to the other, "but you're our best hope."

Bill looked at the other men and back to Fremont, "We'll do our best, Colonel. I think we can make it, but I don't know how long it'll take. It's a mighty long way to go in this weather and with scant rations, but maybe we can get some game when we make the river."

"That's what I'm counting on too, Bill." He reached out a hand to shake the mittened paw of the old mountain man and added, "May God go with you."

"He's sure gonna have to, and we'll be prayin' for you all, too, Colonel."

The men turned away from the fire, going to each camp to secure their gear and ready themselves for the journey. When Bill approached the fire of his camp, Tate stood with his back to the fire and clasping his hands behind him. He looked expectantly to the old man of the woods and smiled, waiting for him to tell what was happening.

"Colonel wants me'n a few other fellas to take on outta hyar and see if'n we can find some relief," he stated as he bent to his pack. Over his shoulder he added, "I ain't so sure of his plan, but I'm thinkin' o' sumpin' you might do, Tate." He turned around and sat back as he looked up at the whiskery face of his friend.

"I'm all ears," replied Tate.

"Me'n the Ute don't get along so well, so me'n these others'll be goin' all the way to Socorro or Taos to try to find help. But, I'm thinkin' if you can make it out an' find a Ute village, you might get help from them. At least you might get some horses, mebbe some pemmican or other food."

"I thought you lived with the Ute for a spell," inquired Tate.

"I did, but it's a long story an' I ain't got time to tell it now. But if you take out soon's you can get away, you'd prob'ly be more help than any of us," proclaimed Bill, lifting his eyes to the younger man. "'Sides, if you hang around here with that horse of your'n, these fellas might get to thinkin' horsemeat'd be better'n mule!"

"Ain't nobody gonna eat my horse!" declared Tate, looking to the trees where Shady stood three legged and dozing. Shady was more of a friend than an animal to Tate, the two had been together through too many trials and battles to become steak on a stick. "I don't know if I can find a Ute village, most of 'em that I know are the Mouache that range farther north, but the Caputa might be around. This is mostly Weenuchiu country. And the Jicarilla Apache hunt up in these mountains, but not in this kind of weather. Yeah, maybe you're right. I think I will try to find some friendlies and get some help."

BILL and his companions were optimistic as they left the wearisome camp behind. The deep snow was a greater hindrance to the others than Bill, with his long legs and lean frame. He chuckled at the others when the snow reached their armpits while he was standing in waist-deep powder. "What seems to be the problem boys? You seem to keep steppin' in holes or sumpin'!"

"If we had long legs and big feet like you, we could walk on top of it too!" declared Breckenridge, holding his rifle over his head as he waded through the snow.

Bill had broken the trail, but with each new footfall, the

lightly crusted snow would give way and the men would sink further. He looked down the steep sided draw and seeing the canyon walls narrow, he turned to the others, "We're gonna hafta climb that ridge yonder, that canyon's too narrow for us to foller the crick."

The men looked where Bill pointed, nodded their heads and motioned for Bill to keep going. By the end of the day, the small group had made what he considered to be five miles. The weary foursome packed the snow down under the branches of a big spruce and made their camp under the protection of the heavy-laden boughs. Bill broke off several dead branches and made a fire and they prepared the scant rations for their supper.

The bitter cold allowed little sleep except in short stretches and come morning the men were even more tired than the night before. As they scrambled to gather their gear, the sugar was spilled out into the snow and lost, leaving them with only tallow candles. Bill looked at the others, motioned for Breckenridge to lead out, and they were soon back in the fight against the snow. Every time he looked up to search for a break in the clouds, he had to brush the wet snow from his face and beard before continuing. This night was a repeat of the one before and gave little relief.

The morning of their third day, Bill was pleased to see the sun peeking over the mountains to their left. As they trudged through the deep snow, the band of daylight worked its way down the far slope until finally he looked up and stared into the face of old sol. It was a welcome sensation after so many days of overcast skies and snowstorms. The mouth of the valley was widening, and he knew they would make the Rio Grande, or as some called it, the Rio del Norte, this day. Their hopes were high as they expected to find game aplenty along the river, and they were salivating at the prospect.

It was a disappointed group that came to the flat beside

the riverbank. Bill looked to the river, frozen over with ice he guessed to be well over a foot thick, and as far as he could see upstream and down there was nothing but white. Trees were humbled by the weight of the wet snows, brush was flattened, and trails were hidden under the deep white. Nothing moved. The men shifted their weight from one frostbitten foot to the other and looked about, hopeful of seeing anything move.

Bill said, "Fellas, we'll camp for the night right down thar," pointing at a pile of driftwood caught at large boulder at the edge of the riverbank. "In the meantime, Breck, you'n King go thataway," pointing upstream, "an' me'n Creutz'll go that-away. Don't go too fer now, y'hear, but see if'n you can find sumpin' to eat, an' we'll do the same. First ones back'll start a fire and make a camp."

Bill and Creutzfeldt returned first, empty handed, and dragged some driftwood to the bank and began a fire, arranging some of the bigger logs around for seats. Bill looked up when he heard the "Hallooo" of Breckenridge and was pleased to see the man carrying a hawk in hand. The scrawny bird was cooked and every edible portion, including the marrow from the bigger bones, was soon consumed by the ravenous men. Their breakfast of that same morning had been the last of the tallow candles that provided little suste-nance until the hawk was downed. But the men found comfort in the fire and slept in a circle around the flames. They found themselves staring at the flames more than sleeping, but the melancholy mood did little to dissipate their hunger and the little snatches of sleep did bring a bit of relief and rest.

CHAPTER TWENTY-SIX
RELAY

"MEN, AS YOU KNOW, I HAVE DISPATCHED OLD BILL AND THREE others to go for help. I'm hopeful they will make it and return as soon as possible. However, I'm thinking that trip will take all of about sixteen days. Now, if we work at it, we should be able to make the river by the time of their return and we'll all be the better for it. You know the mules will be little help, except as food," he looked around as several men groaned at the prospect of more mule meat. He lifted his hand to still the complaints, "and we have a lot of baggage and gear to move. We'll be in three messes, the first I'll lead, followed by the group with the Kerns, and the last and largest group will be led by Mr. Vincenthaler. We will move the baggage as we can and relay it between stops. That's the same as what we've been doing, and it seems to be the only way. So, let's set to and make as much progress as we can." The men began disbursing and Fremont looked to the group, calling, "Mr. Vincenthaler, I would like to speak with you," and motioned the man over.

"Lorenzo, I know I'm putting a lot of responsibility on

your shoulders, but you were with me on the third expedition and in the war with Mexico and I know you to be a good man and a leader. Now, your responsibility will be with the largest group and you'll need to pick up any stragglers or equipment left by the other groups. You might want to split your group and help with the relay of the gear, but I'll leave that up to you."

"I understand, Colonel. We won't let you down," responded Vincenthaler.

As Lorenzo turned away to go to his duties, Fremont noticed Tate standing nearby and apparently waiting to talk to him. "Yes, Tate, is there something you need or a question?"

Tate stepped nearer and began, "I was talkin' with Bill 'fore he left, and he had an idea that might be worth considering."

"Oh, and what would that be?"

"He thought maybe I oughta try to find one of the Ute villages an' see if I can get some help from them. Maybe some horses and food as well. I've been around the Utes, have some friends among the Caputa and Mouache. Don't know if either of 'em have a camp this far south, but it's worth I try I think." He looked to Fremont for an answer and saw the man drop his head to consider his suggestion.

Fremont looked up and said, "He might be right. We need help from any quarter and we certainly can't be choosy at this stage of things. And we certainly don't need a guide to get down to the river, so, yes, I think that would be a good move. You do that, Tate, you do that. And good luck to you!" With that, he turned away, dismissing the young mountain man and starting to pack his own gear.

Tate let a slight grin paint his face and he started back to his camp, already plotting his course out of the mountains and the beginning of his search for the Ute village. Shady lifted his head at the approach of Tate, bobbing it up and down as if he detected the change in Tate's mood, and let a whinny tell of his anticipation. Shady was anxious to be back on the trail and Tate knew his mood matched that of the horse. They both were tired of the inactivity of the camp and even though it meant bucking snowdrifts and cold, anything was better than allowing death and starvation stare them in the face.

Old Bill winced as he put his weight on his frostbitten feet. All the men were miserable and struggled with every step, feeling the prickly pain of the sharp knives of frostbite. With the numbness of their feet, the relentless cold that sought any entry into their clothing, and the stiffness of the leather of their boots, walking was shear agony. Bill was leading the pack and he lifted his eyes to the ice on the river, seeing a dark shape in the middle of the snow topped ice. He turned back to the men, "Can any o' you tell what that is on the ice yonder?"

The men shaded their eyes and squinted against the glare and Breckenridge started at a trot, hollering over his shoulder, "That's a otter! I'm gonna get it!" He sat down and slid down the riverbank, hitting his painful feet on the frozen bank. He winced but kept going, always watching the dark form, holding his rifle at the ready as he walked, agonizing step after painful step. Fortunately, the otter was frozen. He hollered back, "Get a fire goin'!" and began chipping at the body and the ice with the butt of his rifle. He quickly broke it free and started back to the bank. The others had gathered some driftwood and were using the flint and steel to get the tinder smoking. Soon tiny flames licked and caught the kindling, and with Creutzfeldt on hands and knees, puffing on the flames, the fire was flaring.

"Wal, that shore was tasty! A bit gamey, but I ain't

complainin'," said Old Bill as he sat back and pushed his feet toward the flames.

"You're right 'bout that. It was the gamiest meat I ever et, but I ain't complainin' neither!" replied King.

"But what're we gonna do 'bout our feet, fellas. I think we all got frostbite, if they ain't plum froze. I don't think I can go no further like this," pleaded Frederick Creutzfeldt.

Old Bill looked from man to man and down at their feet, "I think if'n we take off the boots, wrap our feet up in strips of blanket, then we can walk. Without that froze leather wearin' on our sore feet, we should make it better. What'chu think?"

Breckenridge answered, "I think you're right Bill. Just the thought of soft warm blankets on my feet makes 'em feel better already."

"But we gotta keep our boots. If'n we don't get nothin' else to eat, we can allus boil the boots and eat the leather," proclaimed Bill. The men looked at him then at their boots, and slowly began removing them. Each man had a blanket and began ripping wide strips from the end and wrapping his feet. Bill watched each one and when all were ready, he stood, using his rifle as a crutch, and started off.

They hadn't gone far when Bill stopped and shading his eyes, looked to the distance, staring and squinting, desperate to make out something, anything that might give relief. The others watched but didn't question the man and he soon started on, all three following. By late afternoon, Bill stopped and searched the far horizon again. He sat down on a big rock and turned to the men. "Fellas, I know this area and the river takes a big wide bend around and turns to the south. Now, I reckon we can cut acrost thataway," he pointed to the southeast, "and save us several miles. It's about fifteen miles 'fore we hit the river again, but it's a lot less than follerin' it around."

"Bill, that sounds alright, but what'chu been lookin' at yonder?"

"I seen some smoke. Probably Utes."

"Utes! That's great! So, why don't we go there and get the Utes to help us. Don't you speak their language?"

Bill sat with his head down, shaking it side to side and slowly lifted to look at the men. "Yes, I speak their language, but I need to tell ya' sumpin'. I lived with the Ute for a good spell when I was a young'un and was even adopted by 'em. One time, cuz I was a white man, they sent me into Taos for some supplies and I had too much to drink. I was fallin' down drunk and the sol'jers made me guide 'em to the Ute village. An' I done it! That was the sorriest thing I ever done, leadin' them sol'jers against muh friends. They kilt a bunch o' them Utes, and cuz o' that, every Ute wants to take my scalp, and rightly so. Terrible thing I did, yessir."

The others were silent as they watched their leader hang his head and mumble to himself. It was a few moments before he lifted his eyes to the three men. Breckenridge was the first to move, standing and walking as short way before he bent down to pick up some twigs. King saw what he was doing and went to the riverbank to fetch some driftwood, as did Frederick. When they had the fire going, that night, they had a nicely browned boot for supper.

TATE's first night out was spent under the same big spruce that made the camp for Old Bill and company. But come morning, the snow and wind drove him back under cover and he huddled with Shady against the cold, making a small fire with some of the branches. The wind whistled and moaned, reminding Tate of his mother when they were back in Missouri. When he was young, she would often scare him with tales of haunts and ghosts, but always ended each tale with a scriptural truth to trust in the Lord. She would also remind him, *And, don't forget Tate, this was just a story, and the idea of ghosts and haunts are nothing more than the imagination of the writers of the stories.* He grinned as he thought of his mother, leaned back against the big spruce, and drifted off to sleep.

CHAPTER TWENTY-SEVEN
HUNGER

FOR TWO WEEKS, THE THREE GROUPS OF MEN STRUGGLED against the weather and miserable conditions of their trek. Fremont's insistence that the baggage and gear be moved was as demoralizing to the group as was the weather. He watched as the men packed as much bedding and gear in the parfleches, and then sent them sliding down the snow packed slopes, sometimes taking out one of the other men that had already reached the bottom. He had to laugh when he saw two men making a race out of it when they packed parfleches and mounted them to slide to the bottom. But even as he laughed, he felt guilty at seeing any humor in their predicament. He had pushed his group to make it to the river and he could see it below. He knew this night would see them camp by the Rio Grande.

9 JANUARY, 1849 *It has been fourteen days since Bill Williams and company started out to find relief. I am afraid they have failed. Whether from the cold, starvation, or savage Indians, I do not believe they will return. The two weeks past have been most miser-*

able. The three messes of men have made progress, baggage has been relayed and our mess made it to the Rio Grande. We are out of provisions and the mules are gone. The men became weary of mule meat, but now would be thankful for more. The other two messes are still in the valley of Embargo Creek and have been forced to take shelter from this never-ending storm. I have seen the men taking rawhide tugs and parfleche hides and boil them for their meal. One mess found some bones and after smashing them to a powder, added them to their rawhide stew to thicken the brew. We cannot continue to survive when all we have to eat are the leathers of the gear. We have resorted to burning books and anything else to get fires started for what little heat we can make.

Vincenthaler has come from his camp and told of finding one of the men, Raphael Proue, frozen beside the trail. I am saddened at the loss, for Proue had been with us on all of our previous expeditions. I believe I will take a few men and mount another rescue mission. If we cannot find Williams, we will push on to find help. I cannot send any more men out into this miserable storm, I must go myself.

--John C. Fremont

THE SUN WAS SITTING off his left shoulder when Tate started over the ridge to the east. When he finally made it to the valley of Old Woman Creek, he reined up and stood in his stirrups to survey the valley for any sign of life. He was hopeful of seeing any game, for it had now been two days since he last ate anything, and that a small handful of pemmican. He dropped back into the saddle and spoke to Shady, "Well boy, what'chu think? Should we go upstream or downstream? I know, I know, there's no tellin' where a village might be, but . . . " and he let his thought drift into the past and the last time he was in this valley. He had come to join Two Eagles and his band for an elk hunt and they met where

Old Woman Creek met the Rio Grande. He remembered Two Eagles saying their camp was further up the valley toward La Garita Creek, but he also remembered the Ute often alternated their camps, seldom choosing the same location for two years running.

As he considered his options, Shady became restless and began sidestepping. Tate reached down and stroked the horse's neck, but he was still anxious. Tate lifted his eyes to the sky and saw the coming storm racing down the valley. He gigged Shady toward the creek bank and a thick cluster of stunted cottonwoods. This was the best shelter available and once in the cluster, he dropped from the saddle and began fashioning a shelter with the branches of a downed tree and others lying around. He worked feverishly and using his canvas groundsheet, he soon had a sturdy lean-to, sufficient for himself and the close growing cottonwoods beside the lean-to would give cover for Shady. Tate dropped the saddle, parfleche, and other gear in the lean-to and began gathering cottonwood bark in a pile nearby. He stripped the dark brown feathery inner bark from the larger pieces. Once he had a good armful, he carried it to Shady who eagerly began to munch on this new feast. He tossed his head in appreciation, and Tate stroked his neck, "See boy, I didn't forget you. Now, what are you gonna get me for supper, huh?"

The storm hit with a fury, but Tate had gathered some firewood and was able to start a small fire on the leeward side of the shelter. He leaned back on the saddle and pulled his blankets around him as he stared into the flames, listening to the howl of the winds blowing the snow through the trees. It was a lonesome sound and he thought of Maggie and Sean, wondering how they were doing. He had hoped to return home in time for Christmas, but that didn't happen, and he knew both Maggie and Sean would be disappointed. And Maggie would be worrying about him. He was confident they were safe and sound with plenty of food and wood for the fire, but he would feel a lot better if he was there with them.

When he awoke, the sun was painting the eastern sky with shades of pink and red. The heavy cloud cover blushed at the brightness of the rising sun and Tate looked around to see almost two feet of fresh snow covering the blankets at his feet. There was no evidence of his campfire and Shady had tromped down the snow at his feet as he looked for any left-overs of the cottonwood bark.

"Alright, alright, I'll get you some more. One of us might as well have something to eat, you haven't gotten me anything, so I guess I better get you some," he complained as he threw the blankets back to rid them of the snow. He gathered another armload of forage for Shady and some firewood for a fire. Even if he didn't have anything to cook, at least the warmth would be welcome. Once the fire was going, he scooped snow into his tin cup and melted the snow and heated the water to have something warm in his belly. He did find a handful of rose hips and chewed on them for something to do, the only taste was bland to bitter and offered little satisfaction.

Once Shady had his fill, Tate saddled up and they took to the trail, pushing the powdery snow and following the hint of a trail north. He knew he didn't have to stumble on the village, just find any sign that told of people nearby. He looked for evidence of trails used, or carcass remains from a hunt, anything that told of people. When he saw some ravens, he made for the area where they circled and called out with their harsh cries. When he neared the area, he saw several of the big black birds pecking at a carcass near the creekbank. As he approached, the ravens scattered, protesting all the while. He dropped down and examined the carcass. It was the remains of a deer that had been dead for some time. There was very little on the bones and nothing to show how the animal died, but with most of the bones still intact, he was certain this deer had probably starved to death. If it had been killed by wolves or a lynx or an Indian, it would have been cut or torn apart, but the ravens and lesser scavengers could only pick the bones clean.

He stepped back into the saddle and reined Shady back to the trail that hugged the ridgetop and stayed just inside the tree line. The snow was not as deep in the trees and it was a little easier going for Shady. Tate was beginning to think this might take a few days to find a camp in this country. He knew they could be just about anywhere as long as they were near water but that did little to limit his search area.

OLD BILL and company had been traveling through the flat lands for five days. Staggering through the snow, fighting the wind and frozen feet. Whenever the sun shined, they suffered snow blindness, but forced themselves to take step after step. Bill was thinking, remembering they had gone through the last of their boots, and now suggested, "Men, try chewin' on yore knife scabbards, mebbe that'll help." They continued pushing and Bill looked back to make sure the men followed. When they could go no further, they stopped and stomped the snow down, making a circle. Once done, they spread a couple blankets on the snow, sat down with their feet in the middle, and pulled the other blankets over their heads as shelter from the wind and tried to get some sleep. There was nothing with which to make a fire and the only warmth was that from one another as they huddled under the blankets.

With the coming of daylight, they forced themselves from their blankets, rolled them up and hung them over their shoulders as pads to carry their rifles. With no game anywhere, they were tempted to leave the rifles behind, but Old Bill admonished them, "Now fellas, when we get to the river, there's prob'ly gonna be more game'n we can shoot. We gotta hang onto our rifles, you know that!" And they continued staggering and limping on towards the river they could not see but hoped was there.

With the wind whipping in their ears, Old Bill heard a feeble cry from behind and stopped to look back. Henry King cried out, "I can't do it! I can't go no further! I will stay here, you go ahead!"

"We can't leave you Henry, now come on, if we can do it, you can," declared Bill.

"No, you go on. I'll rest here and when I can, I will follow!" he demanded.

Bill and the others tried again and again to get him to come, but their arguments failed. Even when they made promises of plenty of game just ahead at the river, he could not be convinced to follow. Bill said, "Alright Henry, you come when you can." He turned to the others and motioned for them to follow and each man reached out and touched Henry on the shoulder as they passed him by and limped away.

The next two hours were the hardest, leaving behind one of their number made each one more aware of his own vulnerability. They crawled as much as they walked, forcing themselves onward. The wavering sight of skeletal trees told of the nearness of the river and the men were revived. Bill stood, leaning on his rifle and looked back to encourage the others. "Come on fellas, we're almost there!" He shouted into the wind and was barely heard, but the uplifted heads told him they knew. He motioned with his arm and turned with the wind at his back and staggered to the drop-off of the river bank.

They struggled to gather wood from the cottonwoods

but soon had a fire raging and they sat as close as the heat would allow. "Now, if we had somethin' to eat, we'd be shinin'!" declared Bill, grinning at the thought. He looked from Breckenridge to Creutzfeldt and saw the latter, head hanging, mumbling to himself. "What's the matter there, Frederick?"

The man lifted his head to Williams with an expression of surprise written on his face and looked back at Breckenridge. Then turned to Williams and said, "I'm goin' back," shaking his head side to side.

"Goin' back? Goin' back where?" asked Bill.

"Back, back to him," and motioned in the direction they just traversed.

"You mean you're goin' back for King? Why, he's dead man, there's no reason to go back."

Breckenridge looked to Bill, "How do you know he's dead?" he asked.

"I seen the ravens. They circle and circle, an' when the circle's real small they drop down. That's cuz they know what they're circlin' is dead."

"I'm goin'!" declared Creutzfeldt as he stood up and started to the riverbank.

"Man, if you go out there, you're gonna join him!" warned Bill. But his words fell on deaf ears as the man climbed the bank and started away at a trot.

Williams and Breckenridge sat silently, soaking up the heat and warming their frost-bitten feet. Bill had taken a short walk up and down stream searching for any game but returned to the fire disappointed and unwrapped his feet to stretch out to the flames again. The last bit of light was fading when they heard the crunch of steps coming down the riverbank. They turned to see Creutzfeldt sliding down the bank and then walking toward the fire. As he reached the circle, he dropped a big chunk of frozen meat onto a flat rock beside the fire. Bill looked at the meat and back at the returnee and said, "Where'd you get that?"

"Found it, dead. Dead, found it!" he mumbled as he plopped down beside the fire, staring wide-eyed.

"You mean you found some dead animal out there? What was it, a deer?" asked Breckenridge as he looked at the long piece of meat. He thought it was the strip from the hind part of a deer's leg.

"Found it, dead. Meat, found it, dead," mumbled the man, still staring into the flames. He looked at the meat, pushed it closer to the fire with his foot and said, "Hungry, eat."

Bill looked at Breckenridge and back at Creutzfeldt. He whispered to Breck, "He's done gone loco. I've seen it b'fore, when fellas are starvin' an' freezin' like we been, it's easy to go loco. What'chu think?"

Breckenridge looked at the man, at the meat, and back to Bill and answered, "I don't think you should be askin' too many questions. You might not like the answers."

Bill looked at the man and back to Breck, "You don't mean . . . "

"Let's just eat. I'm hungry 'nuff to eat a bear that's still fightin', ain'tchu?"

"THE COLONEL LEFT ME IN CHARGE AND HE LEFT DEFINITE orders that we must finish packing the baggage down here to the river. And once we have that done, we are to follow him down the river to the Conejos where he will be waiting with relief!" Lorenzo Vincenthaler, a veteran of the California expedition barked the orders as if he were the commanding general of a troop of green recruits. Doctor Kern had described the man as "a bourgeois soul, crammed with little moralities to make up for the lack of big ones."

The demanding tone of the orders met with grumbling response from the weary cold souls gathered around the large fire at the new camp beside the Rio del Norte, or Rio Grande. Doctor Kern looked around at the haggard faces of the twenty plus men remaining. With almost a month of fighting the blizzards of the mountains and surmounting never-before-seen obstacles of twenty-foot snowdrifts, hurricane force winds, and the untold agony of starvation; these men had lost all hope of relief or survival. He watched as they all, shoulders slumped and heads hanging, shuffled to turn around and look back up the long valley and the trail that was littered with baggage and the refuse of miserable days spent just trying to make it to this river and the possibility of game and fresh meat, only to be disappointed. He lifted his eyes to his artist brothers, Richard and Edward, and asked, "How can we be asked to move baggage when we have used up every last bit of anything resembling food?"

The brothers watched as Vincenthaler pushed his way through the group, forcing his will on the others by pushing them before him and demanding they return to the baggage and bring it down to the camp. Richard looked to his doctor brother, "These men won't last, that's for sure."

"But what else can they do? He's got the orders from the colonel and he alone knows when and where we're supposed to meet up with him," replied Edward.

"But some of these men, if they're not pushed, would just lay down and die!" rejoined the doctor.

"To be honest, I'm about ready to lay down myself," muttered Richard.

Captain Cathcart had walked up beside the brothers and overheard their remarks, "That man is a perfect example of a poor leader."

The brothers looked at their friend, knowing he spoke from experience, having been a captain with the British 11th Hussars. Each of the brothers either nodded his head in agreement or added an 'amen' to the remarks. Cathcart added, "And I fear we will be in for considerable hardship under his lead."

12 JANUARY, 1849 *Have taken Godey and his nephew, McNabb, Pruess and my faithful servant, Jackson Saunders, and am following the river in hopes of finding Williams and company. Left Vincenthaler in charge of remaining men with orders to move the baggage to the camp by the river. It is my hope to find Williams*

and all on their return journey with relief. If they have failed, then we will push on to Taos or any other settlement that may provide a relief party to return for the others. I must gather supplies and am determined to continue to California and will take the Spanish trail in the south.

The wicked weather continues, and our supplies are exhausted. I fear for the men but am hopeful the work of moving the baggage will give them purpose. Our relief column should make the river camp if Williams has made it to Taos. I have instructed the men to follow the river and try to make it to the mouth of the Conejos river for relief. This has been a most difficult endeavor and survival will be a miracle.

-- John C. Fremont

TATE TUGGED on the rawhide belt to tighten it around his shrinking waist. It had been three days since his last food and Shady was subsisting on cottonwood bark and stripped bark from the willows. Last night Tate had pulled his rabbit trick again and made a snow cave under the willows, but Shady spent the night with his tail toward the whistling wind as it blew down the valley of La Garita creek. But now Tate stood back in the trees and facing the rising sun, hoping for some relief from the miserable wind and snow. He shook his head as he saw the veil of white that obscured the morning light and knew there would be no game, not even a rabbit, that would come from cover to face this cold.

He turned away from the dim light and retreated into the trees for some relief from the raging wind. His strength was sapped, but he forced himself to move. Taking several broken branches from the nearby pines, he fashioned another lean-to for a windbreak and started a fire. He slipped the toma-hawk from his belt and began stripping bark from a ponderosa pine. From each piece, he stripped the thin inner bark and started a pile of the white strips. After scooping a pot full of snow and sitting it by the fire, he dropped the strips into the water and stirred them about. Shady walked, with head hanging low, to the side of his friend and watched his working. After several minutes of the boiling water doing its work, Tate dipped several strips, waved them in the air to cool just a bit, and held the handful out to Shady. The horse eagerly consumed the mountain macaroni and lipped Tate's hands for more. But Tate's next handful was for Tate and he began chewing on his first mouth full and gave the remaining bits to Shady. Tate thought the very chewy tidbits tasted just like a pine cone smelled and was almost as sticky. But even though somewhat tasteless, the warm and filling strips made him feel better. Even Shady acted better with his head lifted up as he began walking around the small clearing and pawing at the snow in search of dessert.

He had gone as far north over the many ridges and through the ravines as the narrowing canyon and deep and drifted snow would allow. He turned back yesterday and was bound for the flats where the La Garita opened to the wide valley, in hopes of finding a camp of the Utes and maybe getting some help for the other men. By mid-morning, the sun began to show, and the wind abated enough to lift his spirits and start him back on the trail. The sudden pain in his gut bent him over as he grabbed at his middle. He had never felt this kind of agony and hunger before and the thought that he might not survive made him bury his forehead in the mane of his mount. He had to keep moving, keep searching, anything to make it out of here and back to his family. There was little evidence of any game passing the day before with the drifting snow wiping out all traces of any trail. But the sun pierced the clouds and the blue sky began to show its long-hidden color when Tate and Shady broke from the timber into the flats on the north side of the creek. He slipped the Hawken from the scabbard and checked the load and cap. He rested the rifle across his legs behind the pommel, wanting to be ready for anything, rabbit, deer, elk, or any other game that might provide some fresh meat. That mountain macaroni would not do for a steady diet.

It was late afternoon when he led Shady away from the frozen creek and pushed his way through the deep snow toward a cluster of skeletal cottonwoods. The wider valley of the San Luis showed promise when Tate saw the tracks of deer that had come to the creek earlier. But just as he made it to the trees, he saw movement on the far side of the copse and pulled Shady behind a pair of cottonwood and dropped to his knees. He released the rein, knowing Shady would stand ground tied, and lifted the Hawken to his shoulder, keeping his eye on the movement beyond.

Pushing their way into the clearing before him were five Indians. Tate watched from behind his cover and could make out these were Ute. But with all of them well shrouded in buckskin and blankets, it was difficult to make out any features. When all five had dropped to the ground and began making camp, Tate knew he was too close not to be discovered, and slowly stood, still holding his rifle to his shoulder. Just before he started to call out, he squinted to see a familiar face. "Ho, Two Eagles!"

The warriors turned as one, each grabbing for their weapons and dropping into a crouch as they searched the trees for the speaker. Tate stood, easily dropping the hammer, and lowering his rifle to his side, he started walking toward the men. He had a broad smile when he spoke, "It is good to see my friend," and watched as the grin of recognition crossed Two Eagles' face.

"Longbow! You are far from home! You should be sitting by the fire in your nice warm cabin with your fat wife!" His answering greeting caused his men to relax and lower their weapons as they watched the friend of the people walk into the clearing.

"And you should be in your lodge with your fat wife!" answered Tate, grinning at his friend. He was leading Shady and shifted his rifle to his left hand as he extended his arm to greet his friend. The two men clasped forearms and drew one another close as they chuckled at each other's remarks.

Tate had a little difficulty keeping focused on the conversation as he watched the others preparing some fresh venison steaks and hang them over the fire. His hunger had diminished very little after he and Shady shared their morning fare and his stomach was growling and turning over as he watched the steaks start to sizzle and drip onto the flames. Two Eagles watched his friend drooling over the meat and said, "We will talk more after we eat."

Tate looked back at his friend and realized he had allowed his attention to wane and dropped his head as he admitted, "That meat does look mighty good. It's been many days since my last good meal."

Two Eagles frowned and asked, "Were you with those crazy white men in the high country?"

Tate had to laugh for he had the same thought and even considered himself a bit crazy for giving in to being a part of the expedition. He nodded to his friend as his laughter subsided and admitted, "Yes, I have been with them. I was asked by Old Bill Williams to help them out and have been with them for the last month."

Two Eagles scowled at the mention of Williams and said, "He is no friend of the Ute people!"

Tate was somewhat surprised at the reaction of his friend but when Two Eagles explained about Williams treachery, he understood. "Well, Williams and others already left, but the rest are still in need of help. Would I be asking too much of my friend to bring some horses and food to save these men?"

CHAPTER TWENTY-NINE
BETRAYAL

"It's been four days of abject misery and we still don't have all the baggage down to camp. I'm all for leaving that stuff where it lies and headin' on outta here!" declared Vinsonthaler, feeling just as exhausted as the rest of the men. Just looking at the others he could see despair written on their faces. Starvation was staring them in the face and there was no sign of a relief column as promised by Fremont. The hopeless men didn't even have the strength to stand around the fires, but were seated cross-legged or lying prone, eyes as empty as their stomachs.

"Tabeau and Moran already left!" declared Thomas Martin, his remark eliciting several groans and muttered curses.

Vincenthaler whirled around to look at Martin, "When? When did they leave?!" he demanded.

"Oh, 'bout noon when the rest of us were involved in fine dining on boiled rawhide."

"That tears it!" he declared, "We're leavin' in the mornin', an' if you ain't strong enough to follow, you can stay behind and freeze!"

The Kern brothers were together around another fire. Benjamin, the doctor, looked at his brothers, "Do you think you're going to be strong enough to travel?"

"Apparently, we don't have any choice," answered Richard.

"I do believe that man's intent is to leave most of us behind. He is totally unfit to lead as he is only concerned for himself," observed Edward.

"Well, brothers, we will just have to do as we always have and stick together and take care of one another," pronounced Benjamin.

"I hope you'll include us in your group," came a voice out of the dark. A huddle of six men, Taplin, Rohrer, Andrews, McGehee, Stepperfield, and Cathcart stepped into the light to join the brothers at their fire. Cathcart had spoken and added, "We've little use for that man and have agreed we do not want to be with his group. If you'll have us, we shall travel together."

Benjamin waved his hand for the men to be seated and each one dropped to the packed snow and looked back at Benjamin as if he were the leader. Ben looked from one to the other and said, "I'm no leader, perhaps Captain Cathcart would be best suited for that." He looked at the former British Hussar as the man answered, "I don't think we need a leader. After all, we're just going for a stroll, are we not?" The group chuckled at his understatement and they seemed to relax and stare into the fire.

As EXPECTED, Vinsonthaler and his group departed early and without concerning themselves with the second group under Cathcart. It was soon discovered that the iced over river provided the easiest travel. With less snow and smoother surface, the men, unfit though they were, found travel much easier on the river. Benjamin watched the others, some with frozen or frost-bitten feet, struggle to move. There were as many crawling as walking, with none able to help another. The tall cottonwoods with their skeletal limbs laden with snow and frost took the form of the grim reaper as they stretched their bony shadows across the congealed surface.

A shot broke the silence, but the men barely lifted their heads to see the cause. With no other shots following, they knew there was no danger of attack and they forced themselves to take another step, and another. They came upon a man on the ice, moaning and begging for death. It was Manuel, the California Indian of the Consumne tribe, his feet were badly frozen, and he wanted to die. Ben Kern stopped and examined the man but shook his head as he looked up at the man, "I'm sorry, I can do nothing for you. The soles of your feet are frozen and there's nothing." he shook his head in despair and stood. Joaquin and Gregorio, the other Indians, helped him up and took him back to the first camp.

By late afternoon, the men were exhausted and ready to stop when they came upon the body of Henry Wise, one of the Missouri frontiersmen. He had stopped, sat down, and died. With his eyes open and his face frosted over, he looked like an apparition from the grave. The men kept going just far enough, straggling one at a time and dragging frozen feet, to be beyond sight of Wise and stopped for the night. Word came that the first group had bagged a deer and they were preparing a good meal. The brothers looked to one another and to Cathcart. Andrew had expected them to yield to him and he nodded his head and started for the Vinsonthaler camp.

"Ho, Cathcart! I see your group has finally made it!" greeted Lorenzo Vinsonthaler.

"I understand you bagged a deer. I came for our share of the meat," answered Andrew.

Lorenzo looked at Andrew from under heavy browed eyes and spoke more softly, "We will give you some, however, we are the stronger and need more to keep up our strength."

Cathcart stared at the man, thunderstruck by what he heard, "What makes you think you have the right to play God with other men's lives?!"

"Because I was given that right by Fremont himself when he designated me as the one to make those hard decisions!" spewed the popinjay. Without turning he shouted over his shoulder, "Ferguson! Get their share!"

Andrew heard the bones hit the bottom of the pot and when Ferguson handed it to him, he saw two fore shoulder-blades with little meat and gristle. He looked up at Vinson-thaler and shook his head as he turned away and muttered, "Someday." He walked back to his group and handed the pot to Benjamin Kern, who looked at the bones and back at Andrew with a blank expression, apparently waiting for an explanation. Andrew said, "According to Mr. Vinsonthaler, we of the weaker group do not need the meat as much as they of the stronger group. Since, according to him, we are going to die anyway, we don't need any more." He looked around at the other men and knew what he relayed had hit them hard. But he also thought it would incite enough anger to add to their determination to survive and right now he believed that would drive them further than a few morsels of meat.

The men had settled in to try to get some sleep when they were awakened by the shouting of Carver, "Meat! Meat! I know where we can get meat! Follow me!" He was running around in circles, trying to wake everyone up and rambling incoherently.

When no one followed, he ran off into the darkness as Benjamin called out, "Carver! Carver! Don't go, you need rest!" but the words went unheeded as he disappeared into the darkness.

In the morning, the men were awakened by the smell of meat cooking over the fire. There were small strips of meat sizzling as they dangled from willow sticks and Carver sat staring and licking his lips. He quickly grabbed a strip and began chewing and watched the others approach. He nodded his head and pointed for the others to take some and each one snatched a strip and eagerly consumed the fresh meat.

"Where'd you get it?" asked Micajah McGehee.

Carver just pointed back towards their previous camp and kept chewing, looking somewhat addled and refusing to talk.

"I don't think I'd ask too many questions," mumbled Charles Taplin, happily chewing on the first meat they had in several days.

Micajah looked at Charles and back to Carver and started, "Are you sayin' . . . "

"Nuthin', I'm sayin' nuthin'!"

With only three to four miles made on that day, Carver had showed more erratic behavior than usual. When the men stopped, Benjamin looked towards the man but he jumped up and screamed and ran across the frozen river, struggling through the snowbank, all the while nonsensically shouting and screaming. The others watched him disappear into the night and dropped their gaze back to the fire and the pot of melted snow that held the same bones from the night before. It was only a short while before Vincent Tabeau, often called Sorrell, bent over moaning as he grabbed at his stomach. Doctor Ben tried to help, but the man fell into a violent fit. The doctor explained, "The hunger, cold, exhaustion, snow-blindness, just more than he can take. I think he's given up."

Sorrell's friend, Antoine Moreau, looked from Sorrell to the doctor, "I believe this is a *mise Dieu* (a visitation from

God)." He went and sat beside the prone form of his friend and reached out to give a comforting touch.

In the morning, Benjamin looked at the Frenchmen and motioned for them to come along, but Moreau said, "No my friend, you must leave us. We cannot go further."

Cathcart looked up to see Vinsonthaler walking toward their camp and he stood to greet the man, but a wave of the hand stopped him. Vinsonthaler said, "I'm done! I'm done! It's every man for himself. Maybe if we split up, we'll find more game and be able to survive." Cathcart looked at the man, disgust rising within, and he knew the last remark about survival was only meant to soothe the man's own conscience. He turned away with revulsion showing on his face and motioned to those with him to get ready to leave.

By that evening, the men staggered into camp, one at a time, some dragging in much later. One of the latest was Doctor Kern, who, when he finally came in, fell down and refused to move. He stayed totally immobile for several hours. Some time later, a weak voice was heard back on the trail and when Cathcart responded, he found a very frail and senseless Andrews and helped him into camp. But before he could be roused, the man died. Shortly after, Henry Rohrer, who had been with the other group, stumbled into camp explaining, "I was afraid they would shoot me for meat!"

CHAPTER THIRTY
RELIEF

FIVE DEER STOOD PAWING AT THE SNOW FOR SOME GRASS. THEY were unaware of Thomas Breckenridge, who lay just below the edge of the riverbank no more than a few yards away. So weak, he had crawled on hands and knees for several yards along the river, searching for anything to eat. It was shear effort and determination that enabled him to drag his rifle along. Out of desperation, he scuttled up the riverbank, hopeful of seeing game in the open beyond. Now he carefully peered over the edge, caught his breath, and dared not move.

Ever so slowly, he pulled his rifle up, almost too weak to lift it to his shoulder. He blinked his eyes, trying for a clear shot, scooped up a handful of snow and put it on his almost blind eyes to try to clear his starvation weakened sight. He knew if he missed, Bill Williams, Frederick Creutzfeldt and Thomas Breckenridge would never leave this valley. Quivering with fear and hope, he tried to sight in on the nearest deer, rubbed his eyes again, and slowly brought the front blade into focus and carefully aligned it with the rear buckhorn sight. He slowly squeezed the trigger and the resulting explosion rocked him back and he slid from the bank. He scrambled up as best he could, and the smoke cleared to reveal the one deer down and the white rumps of the others bouncing away.

Leaving his rifle, he crawled to the carcass and slit its stomach open, felt the hot steam of the innards against his face as he reached in for the liver. He pulled it into sight, cut it free and sunk his teeth into the hot meat and chewed like a wolf on its freshly downed prey. It was the sweetest meat he had ever tasted.

He grinned as he leaned back against the carcass, feeling stronger than he had in weeks. The remains of the liver still steaming in the cold air, he started back to the others, thinking of Creutzfeldt who had given up and was waiting to die, and Williams, who sat by his side, waiting for his last breath. He grinned as he walked toward them, knowing his face and beard were covered with blood and not caring, anticipating their response.

Williams saw his friend returning, walking and grinning, and then saw the steaming meat in his hand. Old Bill forced himself up and met Breckenridge, reaching for the meat. He tore into the raw liver, ripping great mouthfuls and chewing with eyes glaring like a madman. He cut a large piece and returned it to Breckenridge, motioning for him to take it to Creutzfeldt. As he chewed on the savory treat, he saw the man who was waiting to die, lift his head as Breckenridge held out the liver. Bill grinned as Creutzfeldt mimicked his own actions and ravenously tore into the raw meat.

Breckenridge sat and watched his friends devour the treat and explained the rest of the deer waited. He suggested they move their camp, such as it was, nearer the carcass to make it easier to carry and prepare. Both men nodded, still chewing, and all three started gathering their blankets and rifles to move nearer their prize which lay on the riverbank just south of the confluence of the Conejos and Rio Grande.

MICAJAH MCGEHEE JUDGED himself to be the strongest of the Kern brothers group and volunteered to try to hunt for some game. He knew he was one of the few that was not snow-blind and although weakened by starvation, he was still stronger than most of the others. He wrapped his feet in blanket strips, remembering how they had consumed the last of the moccasins to little benefit, checked the load in his rifle, and started out in search of anything edible.

Two days had passed since last they ate and that was when Taplin found the remains of a wolf and brought it back to camp. They had roasted the hide and eaten it after making a stew and broth with what little meat remained. Now the ravages of hunger were again taking its toll and McGehee was certain neither Andrews nor Rohrer would probably make it through the next few days.

He heard the coo-cooing call of a prairie chicken and froze, searching the snow-covered sage for movement. He dropped to one knee and watched as a fat bird paraded out from the cover of a sage as if he didn't have a care in the world. McGehee slowly brought his rifle to bear and, wanting to save as much meat as possible, held a steady aim as he squeezed and shot the head off the bird. As it flopped in the snow, Micajah quickly reloaded and had no sooner removed his ramrod than another curious chicken came from a different sage and joined his partner flopping in the snow.

He walked back into camp, proudly displaying his trophies and was welcomed by Benjamin Kern and his brothers and Captain Cathcart. The others were too weak to acknowledge his return with anything more than a weak grin and uplifted hand. Benjamin and Cathcart set about plucking the birds and readying their much-anticipated meal.

When everything, skin, feet, entrails and even pin-feathers, had been consumed, the men turned in for the night. And it would be this night that both Andrews and Rohrer, too weak and dispirited to even share the meal, would succumb to the cold and breathe their last.

———

TATE and Two Eagles rode side by side, each one leading a string of four horses. Two were packed with quarters of elk and two had blankets and parfleche of pemmican. The sun-warmed their backs but made the snow almost blinding. There was a light wind, a pleasant change from the howling blizzards of the days before, and the horses moved easily across the flats. In the valley bottom, where they traveled, the wind had cleared the snow from the grassy flats, leaving strip drifts wherever the taller sage or greasewood provided a windbreak. Tate looked at his friend, sitting proud on his big sorrel stallion warhorse, and asked, "When are you gonna bring that big red over to our cabin and let him have his way with those two mares I got?"

"Ha! Those two scrawny horses could not carry a colt of my horse!" he answered, somewhat smugly.

"I'll have you know those mares are some of the finest bred Morgans around. I know that because the Comanche stole 'em from down in Mexican country, from a well-known breeder and I traded for 'em from their chief, Raven."

"You would do better with mustangs. Comanche do not know horses like Ute!" he declared.

"Say, isn't Red Bird 'bout due to deliver your son?"

"Ah, she is big with child, but she says not til green-up. And is Little Bear big now?"

"That boy gets bigger every day. By the time I get back, he'll prob'ly be goin' out huntin' on his own."

"Ah, we should have a hunt together when the snow is gone. The buffalo will come, and we will hunt together," stated Two Eagles.

"Well, I'm all for that. And if there's anything you can do to make the snow be gone sooner, I'm for that as well."

Two Eagles squinted and stretched out his arm, "There is river. If they follow the river, we will find their sign soon."

Tate stood in his stirrups and shaded his eyes for a better look and said, "Well, even if we don't find 'em right away, I'm all for stopping and giving these horses a rest and us gettin' sumpin' to eat. How 'bout'chu?" Two Eagles nodded his head and gigged his mount forward as they made for the river and the covering cottonwoods.

They sat on a blanket and leaned back against the tall naked cottonwoods, munching on pemmican, and watching the horses paw in the snow for graze. They had checked the frozen river and found sign of several men walking, either the night before or earlier on this day. Two Eagles said, "We will find them soon, before the sun goes down.

"Will you leave these men now and go back to your woman, Morning Sky?" asked Two Eagles of his friend.

"I believe I will, Two Eagles. I'm thinkin' as long as they got horses an' food, they can find their own way down to Taos. 'Sides, I'm missin' my woman and Little Bear."

———

THE SLOWLY DROPPING sun spread its banner of color across the western horizon and silhouetted the San Juan mountains. Fremont shaded his eyes as he looked at the display and felt God was taunting him with the jagged horizon of unconquered mountains. He looked back to see Godey and his nephew Theodore, Charles Preuss, his topographer, and his faithful servant, Jackson Saunders, as they struggled to follow the broken path through the snow that pointed to Fremont. He lifted his shoulders in a heavy sigh as he sought for more oxygen and resolve as he turned to take another step. They were nearing the designated rendezvous point at the confluence of the Conejos and Rio Grande rivers, hopeful they would reach it on the morrow and he was confident they would find Williams and his men.

As he trudged through the unbroken snow, he thought only of those few that followed, proud they had come this far and hopeful they would be fit enough to make the next day's journey. They had been without any sustenance for the past two days and melted snow would not be sufficient for them to go much further. All they had left was two blankets between them, the others having been torn into strips to replace the boots and moccasins that had served as food. He marveled they made it this far and gave a quick thought to those left behind. *Perhaps they have had greater fortune and found game, I pray so,* he thought.

Dusk covered the land when he finally reached the river-bank and slid down the snow-covered slope in search of a suitable camp among the scattered trees and alders. He grabbed at any branches within reach and broke them off to gather some firewood before they stopped moving. He was afraid that if he sat down, he wouldn't have the strength to rise again. Godey matched his movements, gathering branches and sticks for the fire, and hopefully to make a windbreak. With considerable effort, Godey snapped some of the smaller twigs, caught up some of the dry inner bark of a cottonwood and wadded it up for tinder and sat about getting the fire started with his flint and steel.

The smoke started to rise, and the flame began to show when they were startled by, "Halloo the camp!"

Fremont jumped up from the log, rifle in hand and thumb on the hammer when he answered, "Come in if you're friendly!" The sight of the big Ute, sober faced, sitting on the long-legged sorrel that seemed to prance, surprised Fremont and he started to lift his rifle when

Tate rode up beside the Indian and said, "You fellas hungry?"

CHAPTER THIRTY-ONE
SEPARATION

"MR. GODEY, I WANT YOU TO TAKE MOST OF THESE SUPPLIES and those four horses, and you and Mr. Saint, here . . . "

"Whoa up there, Colonel, before you go including me in your orders, there's something you need to know," interjected Tate, sitting on the log by the fire and swirling the hot coffee in his cup.

"What do you mean?" asked Fremont continuing without waiting for an answer, "I am giving the instructions for the day. Mr. Godey, as I was saying, you take these and return to help the others. I'm sure they won't be too far behind. The rest of us, your nephew, Mr. Preuss and Mr. Saunders, we will continue on and gather up Mr. Williams and his men and we will go on to Taos to resupply. I will procure supplies and a detachment to return upriver and intercept you and the others and assist you the rest of the way. Understood?"

"Yessir, Colonel, sir," replied Godey as he started packing up the horses and his gear. Fremont turned back to Tate and said, "Now, what was it you were about to say, Mr. Saint?"

"Well sir, you were including me with Mr. Godey and what you need to know is I am not going with Mr. Godey."

"But those are my orders, you must accompany him," declared Fremont, unused to having his instructions questioned and displaying a touch of exasperation as his complexion showed more color than the snow-burn had given.

"That's just it, Colonel, I agreed to come along on this little journey because Old Bill asked, and I didn't 'sign on' to anything. Now, I've done what I set out to do and that was to show you there was no way a railroad could get through those mountains in the wintertime, as I said at the outset. I left behind a wife and son and I promised them I would do my best to get home by Christmas, but instead I was pamperin' a bunch of men that had no business in those mountains, all because somebody was too stubborn to admit they were wrong. And now, I'm leaving you well supplied and I presume quite capable of finding your path to Taos, cuz all you gotta do is follow that there river, and I'm goin' back to my family. 'Sides that, I haven't done this much explaining since I was sittin' at a desk in the schoolhouse and my own father was the teacher!" He stood and threw the dregs of the coffee into the snow and turned to follow Two Eagles to their horses. Fremont stood, arms crossed on his chest, and watched the two men walk away.

Preuss walked up beside Fremont and said, "Well, Colonel, I reckon he's right. He needs to get back to his wife and child. After all, he did save our bacon, didn't he?"

Fremont looked at his helper and dropped his arms to his side and nodded his head, "Yeah, I suppose he did. So, Mr. Preuss, let's us get to moving and make way for Taos, shall we?"

Once mounted, Tate and Two Eagles reined their horses up beside the other mounts and Fremont. Tate extended his hand, "Colonel, I wish you all the luck and I will remember you and the others whenever I talk to the Lord."

Fremont looked up at the young mountain man and said, "Mr. Saint, Mr. Two Eagles, I am eternally grateful for your timely assistance. I'm not sure we would have made it if you hadn't come when you did." He looked to Two Eagles and added, "I thank you and your people for what you have done. Please relay my thanks everyone."

"I will do that, and may the Great Spirit guide you as you go," said Two Eagles as he shook hands with Fremont. The two friends reined their horses around and moved out of the trees into the flats and were soon out of sight.

28 JANUARY, 1849 *Am now enroute to Taos and believe we will arrive within two or three days. Received horses and supplies from some Ute Indians and hope has been revived. Caught up to Mr. Williams group and dismayed to learn of Henry King's death. I fear there will be others among the other groups as the cold and starvation showed no preference and no mercy. Dispatched Alexis Godey with horses and considerable supplies to bring relief to the other groups and look forward to meeting up with them in Taos.*

The possibility of a railroad route across the 38th parallel does not appear to be realistic. The mountains are impassable, especially in the winter months. I will re-supply in Taos and start again for California on the southern route known as the Spanish Trail. Hope to meet up with my friend, Kit Carson, in Taos. I understand he has a home there and is spending the winter with his bride. Anxious to get back to our property in Mariposa.

- John C. Fremont

"LOOK! Riders! No, just one rider but several horses! Maybe it's help!" shouted Thomas Martin, pointing down the river bank. He stood beside Lorenzo Vinsonthaler and Billy Bacon and looked back to the two to see if they were seeing the same thing. He knew it was not unusual for someone as weak and starving as they were to have hallucinations and imagine strange phenomenon. But both men began grinning and pointing themselves and Martin looked again. He saw a familiar figure on the first horse and said, "That's Godey! He's brought supplies! We're saved!"

The three men grabbed one another and started dancing around in a circle, surprising the others that they had the strength where just moments before they hesitated to take another step for fear of falling into the snow. Their number had dwindled when Scott and Hubbard had dropped out and been left behind. But the remainder watched as Godey came nearer and as he drew close, they could wait no longer when they saw the elk meat on the packhorse. They grabbed at the meat, stripping pieces and putting the raw meat in their mouths as they freed the packhorse of its weight and carried it to the circle that held a fire just hours before.

The next day, Godey and Vinsonthaler, pushed further upstream to find the Kern party and bring them to the lower camp. Godey was determined to rescue all the men that still lived and bring them safely to Taos, but he was saddened to learn that ten men had lost their lives before he could complete his task of rescue.

CHAPTER THIRTY-TWO
HOMEWARD

THEY RODE QUIETLY TOGETHER AS GOOD FRIENDS ARE WONT TO do, comfortable and confident in one another. They crossed back over the Rio Grande, led their horses across the Trinchera and were now moving north, paralleling the wandering Rio Grande. The warm sun shone bright against the cobalt sky and made the wide expanse of snow sparkle, almost blinding both horse and man alike. The horses bobbed their heads, eyes narrowed to thin slits, with each step through the lightly crusted snow that was rapidly melting from the onslaught of warmth. Tate breathed deep of the cool air and took in the pristine surroundings, the first time in weeks that he actually enjoyed and appreciated the wide panorama, after so many days of nothing but blizzard conditions.

Two Eagles saw his friend's actions and spoke, "The same Creator that brought the snow has brought the sun again."

Tate looked sidelong at his friend, "As He always does. But I can't help but think of those that will never see the sun again and lie buried in the snows of the mountains."

"Do not look back, my friend. Let us look before us. We will soon be with our women in warm lodges and thinking about what is to come. We have much to be thankful for, do we not?"

"You're right about that Two Eagles. And one of those things I am thankful for is your friendship. If you had not helped, many more men would have died and perhaps even myself. And for that, and more, I am thankful." Tate looked around and reined up, turning to Two Eagles, he continued, "And now we come to that place where we must go different ways." He motioned with his hand to the northeast for himself and to the northwest for his friend.

Two Eagles gigged his horse nearer Shady and extended his arm and the two friends clasped forearms, pulling each other closer. When they leaned back, Two Eagles reminded Tate, "We are to meet again when the leaves return, and the buffalo come. You will come to our village?"

"Yes, and I will bring Morning Sky and Little Bear. Morning Sky will be anxious to see Red Bird and perhaps by that time you will have your son with you!"

Two Eagles smiled at the thought of his woman giving birth to his first son, "Yes, and that tells me I must soon return to my lodge!" The two men grinned at one another as each reined his horse to the new direction and both raised their open palms to signify the parting of friends.

The flatlands of the San Luis Valley are like many of the plains area flatlands in that they are deceiving in their appearance. To look across the plains, the land does appear to be as flat as a table top, and more so when covered with windblown snow. When the snow is at any depth, the sage and greasewood are covered, and the smooth flatness is exaggerated. But the vast distances camouflage the rolling plains and the many natural dips and rises of the terrain.

Where it appears nothing could be hidden, the low swales obscure the beds of animals or in other seasons, small herds of buffalo or antelope or even warring Indian parties.

It was into one of those dips that Tate pointed Shady as the sun rested on the jagged silhouette of the western mountains. The south-facing slope of the swale was clear of snow while the opposite side held an overhanging cornice formed and frozen by the continual winds. Tate scraped aside the snow in the bottom, gathered enough greasewood and sage to start a small fire as he watched Shady paw at the snow to uncover some bunch grass. The pawing of Shady had startled a snowshoe from the nearby sage and Tate quickly drew his Paterson Colt and secured his supper.

As he sat back and watched the rabbit cook over the fire, he crossed his arms on his knees and began to think about the past Christmas and his family and wondered how he could make it up to them. It would mean more to Maggie than Sean, but his absence would have its price. He pictured Maggie and Sean sitting on the porch and watching for his return and he smiled to himself at the image of his beautiful redhead and her ever present smile. And when he pictured his rambunctious son playing with Lobo or Buster, the bear cub, he squirmed on his seat, anxious to be home with them.

As he lay in his bedroll, hands clasped behind his head and as he looked at the stars, his full stomach reminded him of the many days in the mountains with the expedition when he lay with his stomach growling its disapproval of his neglect. He was still unsettled in his spirit with all that happened on the journey. He knew he had done everything he could for the men, but it hadn't been enough and men died and that bothered him. As he relived those days, over and over again, he thought about what else he could have done and there were no answers. He remembered the words of his father, *Son, sometimes no matter what you do, it won't be enough. All you can do is your best and leave the rest with the Lord. Even then, you'll have questions that won't be answered, especially when you start asking God to tell you the why of things. Sometimes you just won't know until you get to Heaven and He reveals it all to you. Until then, it's a matter of trust.* Yet he struggled with that trust. Some of those men died because they just gave up and others because of the decisions of the leaders, but no matter the reason, they would never see the sun rise again. He focused his thoughts on the stars and then on his family, rolled to his side and was soon asleep.

He followed the tree line that skirted the Sangre de Cristos from the massive sentinel of Mount Blanca northward to the Sand Dunes. It was late afternoon of the third day from Fremont's camp that he came to the trail that crossed Sand Creek and pointed Shady to the well-hidden trail that would take him through the trees to his cabin. He felt Shady quicken his pace as he realized they were nearing home.

MAGGIE AND SEAN sat side by side, Maggie in her rocking chair and Sean on his bench, as they watched the lowering sun start to paint the western sky with the vivid colors that marked the end of another day. Lobo lay at Maggie's feet, head between his front paws and eyes slowly surveying the clearing with only his eyebrows occasionally lifting with the effort. Sean had given up asking his Mom about Daddy's return and he swung his legs back and forth as he looked at his pet wolf. Maggie rested her chin on her palm with her elbow on the arm of the rocker and she looked at the sun, quietly asking *Where are you Tate? When are you coming home? We need you. Oh, please Lord, bring him home safe, soon.*

Suddenly Lobo lifted his head and he rose to his feet, leaning slightly forward, ears pricked, and he began to tremble. He launched himself off the porch and in great bounds crossed the clearing, disappearing into the trees following the unused trail into the shadows. Maggie stood and turned to pick up the Hawken that stood leaning against the logs behind her. She looked to the nipple, saw the cap, and eared back the hammer to full cock, setting the forward trigger. She held the rifle before her and whispered to Sean to move behind. The boy hid himself behind her skirt, peering from the folds to see what had alarmed Lobo.

Maggie was concerned and a little confused, Lobo hadn't growled, nor made any other sound of alarm but he moved as if he were attacking a threat. Two magpies fluttered up from the trees and that gave Maggie warning there was something on the trail that led to the cabin and she dropped to one knee, lifting the rifle to her shoulder as she rested her supporting elbow on her knee and held the rifle at the ready. Something moved in the trees but with the snow-laden branches, Maggie could not make it out. She waited, took in a slow breath, let it out and brought the rifle to bear on the opening between the trees where the trail emerged.

The wolf came bounding out of the trees, tongue lolling, smiling, and looking to the porch. He turned around and looked to the trail to see a horse step into the clearing. Maggie's first thought was the horse looked familiar, then with a good look at the rider, she recognized the capote before she recognized the man. She dropped the muzzle, looked closer, and slowly stood, turned and sat the rifle down to lean against the logs. She looked down at Sean and said, "Daddy's home!"

The boy craned around his mother's skirts, looked up at her smile and back at the man and horse wading through the snow in the clearing and took a tentative step to the edge of the porch. Maggie was right behind him, but they both stopped at the top of the steps and watched Tate ride up to the cabin. He pushed back the hood of the capote and grinning through a whiskered face, "Is it Christmas yet?"

CHAPTER THIRTY-THREE
CHRISTMAS

ONE STEP TOOK HIM TO THE TOP OF THE STAIRS AND BESIDE HIS Maggie. He wrapped his arms around her and lifted her up with her feet kicking behind her and they kissed one another passionately. When he lowered her to her feet, the jerking at the fringe on the side of his leggings told of another that wanted some affection. He turned and picked up Sean, hugging him as they spun around in a circle. Maggie grabbed his arms and slipped them back around her waist as she tiptoed and kissed him again. All three were laughing and crying and dancing around in the circle of excitement and happiness.

"Oh, it's so good to see you two again!" declared an excited Tate, with a grin splitting his face. He dropped to one knee and drew Sean near as Maggie sat back in the rocker, refusing to let go of his other hand.

"Well, you sound like my husband, and you have on my husband's clothes, but you sure don't look like him!" she declared.

"Momma, it ith too Daddy, I know!" interjected Sean as he held on to his daddy's knee.

"Well, I'm thinkin' he's going to have to get rid of all that," pointing to his facial whiskers, "before I'm sure. Our daddy didn't have all those whiskers when he left!"

Sean reached up and ran his hands through the whiskers, "Yeth, they're stickery!" He scowled at the feel of the beard.

"Well, you two look mighty good to me and I'd recognize you anywhere! And I do believe," started Tate as he looked at Sean, "that your Momma is even prettier than she was when I left!"

"Yup, she ith! An' sheeth got a secret!" declared the boy, grinning up at his mom.

Tate looked from Sean to Maggie, "A secret? And what's this big secret?"

"It's a secret, silly. If we told you, it wouldn't be a secret anymore, now would it?"

"All right, well, you two just keep your secret. But, one thing that's not a secret is that your daddy's hungry! Have you had supper yet?"

"Uhn uh, not yet," answered Sean, looking to his mom.

"Well, I've gotta tend to Shady and then I'll be right back. How 'bout you helpin' your Ma get us some supper ready, alright?"

"Umhumm," answered the boy as he walked to the rocking chair and took his mother's hand to pull her up. "Come on, Mom, leths fix thupper for daddy!"

She smiled and stood and motioned for Tate to get along to the corral and she walked into the cabin. She replaced her capote with an apron and went to the counter to cut some meat cubes and potatoes to add to the pot of stew cooking at the fire. She started a fresh pot of coffee and pushed it nearer the flames.

With a rush of cold air, the door opening revealed a heavy-laden Tate who kicked the door shut and dropped his armload beside the door. He shivered out of his capote, removed his jacket and hat, and stepped to the fire to extend his hands to the warmth. He turned around to get some heat on his backside and saw the Christmas tree in the corner. A broad smile painted his face and he looked to Maggie, "That's special!" nodding toward the tree. It had been decorated with popcorn strings, trade goods of tin bells and beads, pine cones and a carefully crafted angel on the top. Some of the needles had dropped off, but he saw the bucket that held the tree stable and knew Maggie had kept the tree watered for it to last this long. He shook his head as he thought of all she had done while awaiting his return.

"I sure wish I'da been here!"

"Oh, we haven't had Christmas yet. Somebody was missing!" she declared.

As they gathered at the table, Tate stretched out his arms and clasped hands with Sean on one side and Maggie on the other. They bowed their heads and Tate gave thanks to the Lord for bringing him safely home, keeping Maggie and Sean safe in his absence, and His many other blessings. It was a very thankful family that bowed their heads, and thanked their Lord for all He had done for them. At the group "Amen," Sean said, "Leth eat!" and Maggie and Tate laughed at their eager son.

After finishing their meal, Sean looked to his mother and asked, "Can we open 'em now?" as he ran to the tree and pointed at the presents underneath. He looked back at his Mom and Dad and jumped up and down in excitement.

Maggie looked at her son, over at Tate, and back at her son and said, "First, your father has to read the Christmas story!"

"Pleath?" pleaded the boy as he ran to his father and looked up at his whiskery face.

"Sure," replied Tate as he stood and went to his pack to retrieve his Bible. He sat down at the table and motioned for

Sean and Maggie to join him around the table that held the candles. After everyone was seated, he turned to Luke 2 and began reading the Scripture that told of Jesus' birth. When he saw Sean beginning to nod, he finished his reading with verse 11 *For unto you is born this day in the city of David a Savior, which is Christ the Lord.* He closed the Bible with an "Amen."

Sean looked up excitedly and said, "Now?"

Maggie smiled and laughed, "Now!"

Sean ran to the tree and grabbed a package wrapped with colorful gingham and brought it to Maggie and she handed it to Tate. "Get the other one like this," she instructed the boy. He ran back and retrieved a smaller package that was wrapped just like the other one and brought it to his mother. She laid it by the chair the youngster used and motioned for him to open it. Sean jumped in the chair and grabbed the package and began opening it, giggling all the while. As he busied himself, Maggie motioned to Tate to open his.

The excited boy brought out a pair of leather mittens but was confused as he looked at his mom. She took the mittens and put them on his hands and he smiled broadly and waved at his daddy across the table, who held up a matching, but much larger pair. He watched his daddy put his on and smile and clap the mittens together, and Sean mimicked his father, joining in the muffled clapping and giggling.

Tate looked at Maggie and said, "These are very nice, but they're not rabbit fur, what are they?" He took them off and rolled back the cuff and looked at the fur, frowned and held them closer to the light and felt the fur and looked at the mottled color and up at his wife. "Is this . . . ?

She grinned at him and nodded her head. "And it wasn't easy getting that tanned with the hair on, either!"

"But, how did you . . .?" he started as he looked with wonder at his wife.

"Well, Sean and I went looking for a Christmas tree, and . . . " she began and related the story of how she, with the help of Lobo, bagged the Lynx that wanted to make a meal out of Sean. "And then I had the idea to make mittens out of him!" She smiled smugly at her wayfaring husband, "and I cut slots for your trigger finger and thumb, so you don't have to take them off to reload or shoot!" She showed her handiwork to Tate as he continued to stare at his independent wife.

He shook his head and smiled as he looked at her and said, "And here I was worried about you! I reckon it's the animals of the woods I shoulda been worried about." He got up from his seat and walked to his packs and began rummaging through the stack. He stood, holding his hands behind his back and returned to the table. Both Sean and Maggie looked wide-eyed at him and he brought one hand around and extended it to Sean, holding a well-crafted bow and three small arrows. Sean's eyes grew wide and he slowly reached out to accept the proffered gift, glancing at his mother for her approval. Maggie's smile and nod encouraged the lad as he accepted the extra-special gift. Then Tate brought the other hand around and held a beautiful beaded necklace that he offered to his wife.

"How did you . . . "

He smiled at her response and explained, "When I went to Two Eagles village, I did a little trading."

The beaded necklace, in shades of blue with white designs, lay flat against her neck and hung below her throat with a wide pattern and trailing edges. She stroked the artful piece as she looked at her husband. He was watching the boy as he ran his fingers over the small bow. It was the perfect size for the youngster and would serve to teach him how to safely use what essentially was a weapon. But it would give him an opportunity to learn and develop a skill that would serve him well in the wilderness. He looked to his momma and smiled as he held up the bow, "Look Momma, Daddy give me a bow! And arrows!"

She smiled and nodded her head, "Isn't that wonderful! Maybe tomorrow he will show you how to use it!"

"Or your Momma could. She knows how to use one of those too."

"Bof of you!" declared the boy as he stood and took the bow to his father. "Fith it!" as he held out the bow and string. Tate easily bent the bow to attach the string, pulled on it carefully and said, "See there, that's all you do. But, you can't use the arrows until we get outside, understand?"

"Ummhumm," answered the excited boy. With bow in hand, he began running around, drawing the bowstring, and making sounds as if he were shooting an arrow at passing animals. "Got him! Got that lynnngth!"

Tate rocked back and laughed, "Just like your momma!" He looked at Maggie and said, "So, what's this secret?" as he grinned at her and took her hand in his, looking at her candle lit face that showed a touch of mischievousness. He had always enjoyed that about his Irish wife, how she could find pleasure and fun in even the simplest things and could bring a bit of joviality to any event.

She turned to face him and smiled, using both hands to grasp his larger calloused hand and looked into his eyes and asked, "Will we go to Red Bird's village in the Spring, you know, when she is ready to deliver their child?"

Tate frowned at the question, but answered, "Yes, we talked about getting together in the spring and go on a hunt. Actually, he said, when the leaves come and the buffalo return. But that's about the time Red Bird should have the child. Why?"

"Well, I wanted to be there for her and then she could be here for me."

His eyebrows dropped, and he cocked his head to the side, "What do you mean?"

"You know, when my time comes." She smiled and turned her head away, trying to keep from laughing at his consternation.

"Now you've got me confused. What are you talking about?" he asked as he leaned back and examined her expression.

Sean had stopped to listen and now lay his head on his momma's lap, then stood up and looked at his dad and said, "I'm gonna haf a thister!"

Tate scowled as he looked at his son, then lifted his eyes to Maggie and asked, "Did he say . . . " and the nodding head of Maggie and her beginning giggle as she put her hand to her mouth answered his question.

Tate jumped to his feet and rounded the table in two quick strides and lifted Maggie to her feet and wrapped his arms around her to bring her close as he bent to kiss his sweetheart. He pushed her back to look into her eyes and said, "When?"

She laughed as she said, "Oh, late summer I think."

"How do you know it's a girl?"

She chuckled and said, "Oh, I don't know, I just do!"

Tate picked her up again, kissed her again, but was interrupted by Sean, "Me too, Daddy!"

"Wow, what a homecoming!"

Cabin fever is a common malady for those in the mountains enduring long and difficult and often unrelenting winters. When the bitter cold and deep snows limit outdoor activity, there is only so much that can be done indoors. With no furniture to make, all harness and gear repaired, all the guns cleaned several times, Tate's restlessness became bothersome to everyone in the household.

"Why don't you take Sean outside and start teaching him how to use that bow?" declared a slightly exasperated Maggie as she worked the needle and thread through the material she was fashioning into an infant's gown. "If you don't do something to get the two of you out from underfoot, I'm going to have to go outside myself just to have some peace and quiet!"

Tate lifted his shoulders with a deep sigh and looked to his son, sitting in the corner and playing with the wooden horses carved by his father. The horses were just a few of the carvings that Tate had used to occupy himself over the last five or six weeks. He stood and bent over to ask Sean, "So, whaddya say son, you wanna go outside and shoot your bow?"

The youngster jumped to his feet and shinnied up the ladder to fetch his prized bow and arrows that had lain dormant since his mother's orders to "Put them away. You're just going to have to wait until the weather's better and you and your father can go outside!" He was excited the day had finally arrived when he and his father could venture outside, and he could learn to master the skill of shooting his bow. "Pa!" he called as he leaned over the loft rail. He motioned with the bow for his father to catch and dropped the bow and arrows, now tied together, into his uplifted hands. He came down the loft ladder with practiced ease, his coat and mittens over his shoulder. His coat was a copy of his fathers with rabbit fur lining and antler buttons and his mom had made him a cap with ear flaps from the rest of the lynx pelt. As soon his feet hit the plank floor, he started donning his outside gear and watched his father do the same.

Maggie set down her sewing and finished buttoning up Sean's coat, and slipped on his mittens. She demonstrated how to flip back the end of the mitten and bring his fingers out to use for his bow, then tucked his hand back in, and pulling up his fur collar and pulling down his ear flaps. She looked to Tate and said, "Now, you bring him inside if he starts to get too cold, y'hear?"

Tate grinned at his protective wife and chuckled, "I know, I know. But us men won't get cold, will we son?" he declared as he looked at the boy with only his cherubic face showing. "Are you sure he's gonna be able to even move the way you've got him bundled up?"

"He has to stay warm! He doesn't have all that winter fat that you do to keep him warm!" she jibed as she nodded to his belly that pushed at the antler buttons of his buckskin shirt. Since he had been home, the inactivity of the indoors and her good cooking had not just replaced the weight he lost on the expedition but added to it considerably.

When they stepped onto the porch, Tate went to the rail and stretched himself tall, extended his arms and sucked in a deep breath of the early spring air. He chuckled as he saw Sean mimic his actions and breathe deep as well. "Ahh, that fine mountain air! So fresh and smellin' of pines and freedom! Ain't that great son?" he asked as he looked down at his miniature self.

Sean looked up at his father and smiled as he nodded his head. "Ummhumm!" not fully understanding but happy to be together with his dad. "C'mon Pa, let's shoot!" he shouted as he started down the stairs, taking one long step, pausing, then another.

The clearing before the cabin was free of snow but the nearby trees sheltered some drifts that, hidden from the sun, would last until well into spring. It had been most of three weeks since the last bit of fresh snow and now the pines and spruces were showing new growth at the tips of their branches, giving a more pungent and pleasant scent to the air. The valley below was beginning to show the first sign of green, although the gullies still held snow drifts. The mountain streams were beginning to run as the last bit of ice melted away and the snow from up high was starting to lose its grip on winter. It would still be some time before the aspen began to bud, but spring was pushing back the winter and would soon clothe the mountains and valleys in the green of new life.

Tate followed his son down the stairs and led him to the woodpile to secure a piece of split wood for a target. They set it up, supporting it with a couple of rocks, and walked back about fifteen feet. "Now, let me show you how to string your bow," he began. He demonstrated placing the lower nock of the bow by his foot, using his knee to bend it for the string to reach the top and slip into the nock. "There, see?" then bent the bow to release the string and said, "Now, you try it."

Sean looked at his dad questioningly and started the process as Tate knelt beside him. The boy struggled at first, but with a little help from dad, he succeeded. He turned and smiled, "I did it!"

"Yup, you sure did. Now, here's the next part," pointing at the grip he said, "Take hold of right here, that's it," he encouraged as the boy took a firm grip. "This right here, the little shelf right above your hand, that's where you rest the arrow as you take a sight. So, let's try it."

Tate handed an arrow to the boy who quickly nocked it on the string and rested it just above the grip. "Now, here," pointing to the nock of the arrow and the string, "You always make sure this part of the fletching has the feather away from the string so it won't hit the grip and tear off, you see?"

"Ummhumm, I see."

"And you hold the string, not like your pinching it, but with two fingers above and two fingers below the arrow nock," he maneuvered the boy's fingers to the suggested position. "When you lift the bow, put the thumb of your shooting hand out to touch your cheek," he lifted the bow, "And look right down the shaft to your target. When you have the target in line, pull back on the string and check your sight again." He watched as the boy stiffened his arm, pulled back on the string and sighted down the arrow and let it fly.

"I hit it!" he declared as he jumped up and down, looking at his father. Tate grinned at the boy, "You sure did! Now, try it again!" He watched as Sean picked up another arrow and quickly nocked it, checked the fletching position, and began to draw back on the bow to sight his target. He quickly let another arrow fly and again hit the target. He looked up at his father, grinning with pride, waiting for praise, and was not disappointed.

Tate returned to the steps and sat on the top step to watch Sean as he practiced. Lobo lay down on the porch, his head next to the elbow of Tate and both watched the youngster as he repeatedly shot the arrows, fetched them back, and shot again.

"Now, step back a little more, back this way," called out Tate and watched as Sean made the distance to the target about twenty feet. He tried again and again, but at this distance he found it a little more challenging to hit the target. He was drawing back the arrow when he quickly lowered it as Lobo lifted his head and growled. Tate stood and looked to the trees, knowing something had alarmed the wolf. He called into the cabin, "Maggie, bring my rifle." The door slipped open and her hand extended the Hawken to her husband as she held the door open just enough to view the clearing. Tate motioned for the boy to come to the porch and he quickly mounted the steps to stand behind his father.

A string of six animals, the first three mounted, were led by a familiar figure that brought a smile to Tate's face. "Well, if it ain't Old Bill Williams! What in the world are you doing back in these mountains? I'da thought you had enough of this country!" he said as he set down his rifle and moved down the steps to greet the visitors. He stood, hands on hips, as Old Bill reined up his horse beside him. "Come on and step down," he said as he motioned to all three men. He didn't recognize the others, noting they were Mexican and were leading pack mules, one of which had a pack while two just carried pack saddles and obviously empty panniers.

"I reckon you are lookin' for a good woman cooked meal, am I right?"

"Yup, you're right about that," then looking at his host he added, "And from the looks of things that woman's cooking has agreed with you!"

Tate patted his middle and answered, "Ain't none better.

But I reckon after you tryin' to starve me to death, I kinda took to overeatin' just in case I come on lean times again."

Maggie came out on the porch and watched the men as they greeted one another, and she stood with arms crossed as she listened to them talk about her cooking. "And I expect you'll be wanting more of that good cooking?" she kidded, with a broad smile that showed her brilliant white teeth.

Old Bill doffed his hat and bowed slightly at the waist, "Howdy Maggie! And yes, the thought of your fine cooking certainly has my mouth watering!"

"Well, you tend to your animals and I'll get something started," she answered, turning to the doorway with a wave over her shoulder.

LITTLE WAS SAID during the meal with the exception of small talk about the times and the weather. It was only after Sean had been sent to the loft for an afternoon nap, and Juan and Jose, the Sanchez brothers, were sent to ready the animals that Bill and Tate began to talk in hushed tones. "So, how did things work out?" asked Tate.

"Well, not too bad, I reckon, all things considered," answered the long tall elder of the mountains.

"How many?" asked Tate, inquiring about the number of dead.

"Ten," answered the sober Bill. "Let's see, there was Proux, the Frenchman you knew about. Then King that was with us, Henry Wise, Sorel and Moran, then Carver, Andrews and Rohrer. After that was Beadle and Hibbard. All of 'em starved or froze to death," dropping his head and shaking it side to side. "Hard times they was and we'd best forget 'em, yessir, forget 'em for sure. But I don't think I ever can, done some things muh own self I ain't too proud of and don't like goin' back. But Fremont, wal he already headed out to Californy via the Gila route and he wanted me to try to recover any o' the gear left behind and to bury the remains of any we find. Ain't doin' it fer him, but fer them fellers whut fell cuz o' the stubbornness and stupidity of others." He shook his head as he stood to leave. He looked at Tate and said, "You be mighty lucky havin' a fam'ly like ya' got. You be right sure to take care of 'em no matter what, y'hear?"

"Oh, I know Bill, I know. What we shared up on the mountain made me appreciate what the good Lord has blessed me with and I don't think I'll ever be separated from 'em again."

Bill put his hand on Tate's shoulder and said, "Don't ever forget what happened up yonder, but at the same time, do your best to put it outta yore mind, or it'll come back to haunt you. I know you didn't have to experience much o' what the rest of us did, cuz you was out by yourself tryin' to look out fer the rest of us, but what the rest of us done, wal . . . " and he let the subject drop as he shook his head walking to the door.

Tate followed his friend out and shook hands after the old man mounted up on the big strawberry roan gelding. He stroked the neck of the beast as he looked up at the elder statesman of the mountains and advised, "You keep your topknot on, y'hear? Them Utes still got a bur under their blanket 'bout'chu."

"I know, I know, but them fellers need buryin' and I aim to do it right. Read over 'em from the Scriptures an' all. Needs to be done an' I'm the one to do it," he declared as he reined his mount around and motioned to the brothers to follow. He turned and waved to the couple standing arm in arm on the porch and called back, "May the Lord bless you and yourn!" Tate and Maggie waved in return and watched them leave the clearing, headed for the valley and the mountains beyond.

CHAPTER THIRTY-FIVE
VILLAGE

"You look worried, what's weighing so heavy on you?" The words came from the redhead, rocking on the porch as she looked at her man seated on the top step and running his hand through the scruff of Lobo's neck.

Tate bobbed his head as he turned to look at his concerned wife, "Oh, I dunno, guess I was just thinking of Old Bill. It's been three weeks now and I thought he would have come back through and stopped by after his trip to the mountains. Not like him, he's one that likes to visit and talk over old times."

Maggie nodded her head as she rocked, "Maybe he didn't have the time, I s'pose Fremont was anxious to get all that gear that was left behind."

"That's just it, Fremont left for California before Old Bill stopped here. I s'pose he could ship it to him, but no tellin' how much stuff he was able to salvage. He just seemed, well, bothered, when he was here. What happened on that expedition seemed to be haunting him, an' that ain't like Old Bill. He's been through more'n most men even think about, an' I never thought anything'd bother him, but . . . " and he let the words drop as he became introspective and thoughtful.

Suddenly Lobo jumped to his feet, ran to the end of the porch and looked to the woods. He spun around, went down the steps in one bound, and ran lickety-split to the trail that wound across the mountain into the thicker timber. Within moments he was back and running for all he was worth into the clearing as a big ball of brown fur loped after him. Tate jumped to his feet and grabbed his ever-present Hawken, checked the nipple for a cap and brought the hammer to full cock. He lifted the rifle to his shoulder as he watched the two fur balls chasing each other around the clearing, growling and barking.

A grin slowly spread across Tate's face as Maggie stood beside him pulling on his shirt sleeve. They looked at one another and back at the clearing, and Maggie turned to the door to call the boy. "Sean! Sean! Come see."

Within moments the boy pushed his way through the door, rubbing his sleepy eyes and asked, "What?" Maggie pointed to the clearing and Sean instantly became wide-eyed. He looked to his mom and asked, "Is that . . .?"

Maggie nodded with a wide smile at her son and watched as he went to the top step to watch the two friends, one grey and one cinnamon colored, chasing each other around the clearing. Sean turned back to his mom and dad saying, "He's bigger!"

"You're right about that, son," answered Tate. The entire family was getting a special thrill out of the antics of the two furry friends, when Lobo flopped down, tongue lolling to the side, and the big bear sat down on his rump and then dropped to his belly. Both were exhausted, and Sean started to go to them, but was stopped by his dad.

"No, no, we'll need to wait until Buster approaches us. We

have to make sure he remembers us. It won't take long, I'm sure. Let's just sit down here and watch."

And Tate was right, when Buster and Lobo rose from their rest, the bear went straight to the steps to greet the boy and his dad. Maggie had gone into the cabin and returned with some meat trimmings that she handed to her men to feed the returning bear and Lobo. She could tell by the expression on the two friends that they were happy to be back together. And Sean, now quite a bit taller than when Buster went into hibernation, was still dwarfed by the bear, who had also grown.

"So, now that he's back, are we going to take him with us to Red Bird's village?" asked Maggie, getting anxious for the trip to see her friend.

"Sure, why not? I think they'll be alright together, and we'll keep an eye on 'em. Now that we have Big Bear back, Little Bear's gonna be hard to keep close."

Sean grinned at his father's use of his Indian name and buried his face in the neck fur of the bear and turned back to his folks, "Little Bear's glad to have Big Bear back, too."

"So, how long will it take us to get there and when are we going?" queried Maggie.

"Oh, I reckon we oughta start gettin' ready. Two Eagles said, 'when the leaves come and the buffalo return' and I noticed the aspen are showin' their buds and I'm sure the buffalo will be showin' up anytime now."

Those were the words Maggie had been waiting to hear and she jumped up from the rocker and into the house to begin her preparations. Although there wasn't much to do for she had been planning and preparing for this trip since Tate returned and spoke of it. Having organized everything in her mind, several times over, she was quick to pack the parfleche and the panniers that sat by the door.

Tate had been using his time and pent-up energies tending to the animals and their gear, so there was little for him to do as well. With the horses all getting several brushings and trimmings, all he needed to do was get the gear organized and laid out for the morning departure. He led them all down to the pasture just below tree line, Sean and the two fur friends trailing, and staked them out for a good graze. After a couple hours of grazing for the horses, running and chasing for Lobo, Buster, and Sean, Tate gathered all together and started back to the cabin.

Maggie was sitting in her rocker awaiting their return and smiled as they entered the clearing. Tate put the animals in the corral and motioned for Sean to go to the cabin. Lobo and Buster found their place on the porch and stretched out for a time of rest, while the family went inside for their supper. Everyone was in high spirits and even the animals seemed to know something was in the wind.

COME EARLY MORNING, Tate led the other horses to an upper meadow he had made into a big corral, the same where Maggie's mare had been killed. He knew they would have plenty of graze and water and would be as safe as possible during their absence. When he returned to the cabin, Maggie and Sean were anxiously waiting. Maggie had saddled her dapple-grey mare and the panniers and parfleche were on the porch. Tate smiled and chuckled, "So, why didn't you rig up the packhorse while you were at it?"

"Oh, I thought I'd leave something for you, so you'd feel needed!" she grinned.

Within moments, Tate led the piebald packhorse to the porch and loaded her up. Sean would swap off riding with Tate and Maggie, at least for another year, until he was old enough to capably handle the steel-dust colt that he claimed. With everyone and everything aboard, the family started through the timber, planning on taking a straight-line across the valley floor to the far mountains that held the Ute village.

Tate knew they could make the journey in two days, but with the ever curious, let me look, smell, and taste everything Buster along, he chose to make it a more leisurely three days. It was mid-afternoon on the third day when they rode up the La Garita Creek valley to the recently settled summer camp of Two Eagles' village. The horse herd of the people was lazily grazing on a small meadow below the camp and Tate reined up to look a little more closely. He turned back to Maggie asking, "You remember the horse Old Bill was riding when he stopped by our cabin?"

"Yes, it was a big strawberry roan, wasn't it?"

He turned toward the herd and pointed, "Look over there on the left side, by that big black. Doesn't that look like Old Bill's horse?"

Maggie stood, tip-toed in her stirrups and moved side to side for a better view and answered, "Yes, it does," and turning to Tate with a smile, "Does that mean he's here? Maybe that's why he didn't stop back by the cabin."

"Uh, no. He won't be here. If that's his horse, and I think it is, that means Old Bill won't be stopping by anywhere."

"What do you mean?" asked a furrowed brow redhead.

"Oh, it's a long story. I'll tell you after we get settled."

With the entourage of three horses, one wolf and a bear, Tate had Maggie join him as they led the group into the village. Sean was mounted on Maggie's dapple grey and Lobo and Buster walked between Tate and Maggie. As the people of the village waved and shouted their welcome to the expected friends of the Ute, many looked somewhat surprised to see them accompanied by both a wolf and a bear, but many of the ever curious and excitable children rushed forward for a better look, and hopefully a chance to play with the animals.

"Greetings my friends," came a familiar voice as Two Eagles and Red Bird came from between two tipis. Their friendly smiles were a welcome sight and the good friends greeted one another, Maggie with a hug of Red Bird, and Tate and Two Eagles clasping forearms. "We have a lodge for you while you are with us. Come with us," directed Two Eagles as he turned to lead the way. Maggie and Red Bird were already chattering excitedly about the impending event of her first child's birth.

While the women settled the gear in the tipi and Sean played with the animals, Tate and Two Eagles took the horses to the herd and on the way, Tate asked Two Eagles about the roan.

Two Eagles stopped and looked at his friend, "Yes, that is the horse that belonged to the man you called Old Bill. For many years, he was the enemy of our people. He had betrayed our people and caused the death of many."

Tate dropped his eyes to the ground, sighed heavily, and looked to the herd and started walking, leading his horses. Two Eagles walked beside his friend and stopped when Tate slipped the headstalls and halters from the horses, to turn them in with the herd. Tate walked to the roan, who lifted his head expectantly at the sight of the white man and stroked his head and neck without saying anything. He stepped back and looked to Two Eagles, "Old Bill told me what he did and that it weighed heavy on him all of his life. He was very sorry but knew he could do nothing to change it and he believed that one day it would cost him. He stopped by my cabin before he went back to these mountains and we talked a little."

Tate and Two Eagles started back to the village, "He was going back to find the bodies of those that died on our expedition and to bury them properly." He turned to Two Eagles to ask, "Is that where it happened?"

There were a couple of moments of silence between the friends and Two Eagles nodded his head, "Yes, it was a hunting party led by Lone Bull and Broken Bow. They knew of this man, their fathers were killed in that attack, as was the brother of my father."

As Tate listened to Two Eagles' explanation, he knew he could not fault him nor the men that killed his friend. The people believe that if a warrior is killed, he cannot rest on the other side until his death has been avenged. It had been many years since the betrayal, but it had not been forgotten by those who lost loved ones and family.

While both white men and the natives believe in an afterlife, to the natives it is more than a belief, but a way of life. The people look forward to the afterlife, preparing themselves for it according to their beliefs and during a time of battle with their enemies, they do what they can to prevent their enemy from going to or enjoying the afterlife. That is why they mutilate the bodies of their enemies, cutting out their eyes so they cannot see in the afterlife, cutting off their hands, ears, and disemboweling them so they will be handicapped on the other side, unable to enjoy that spirit world. The white man just hopes there is an afterlife and that they will go there. Some believing it enough to spiritually prepare themselves but never believing that by mutilating the body of another, they could prevent anything.

After the meal with their friends, Maggie put Sean to bed in the lodge and returned to the small fire outside to sit and talk with her man. She knew something was bothering him, but she waited for him to share and she didn't have to wait long. They sat side by side staring into the flames and he turned to her, "Maggie, I've got somethin' I've gotta do . . . " and began explaining about the death of Old Bill. He told of the betrayal and of Bill's burden and belief it would be his undoing. He told of the deaths of many of the people and their belief in vengeance for the peace of those that were killed. "Those that killed him were sons of those that died because of his betrayal. Two Eagles told me where it happened, and I need to go and bury him and read from the Book. You understand, don't you?"

"Yes, I do. Do you want me to come with you?"

"No, I figgered you an' the boy could stay here, Lobo and Buster too, and enjoy the time with Red Bird. She was mighty excited to see you and to know you would be here with her. It shouldn't take more'n a couple days. It ain't too far." He had spoken in soft tones and with bowed head, showing the heaviness in his spirit and the burden of the obligation to see to his friend's burial.

Maggie reached out her hand and covered his, "Of course, you'll go. We'll be just fine here in the village and you'll be back soon. I understand."

He lifted his head and smiled at his redhead and pulled her to him. They held the hug for a long time, enjoying the moment and sharing the loss. When they pulled apart, Maggie noted a small tear escaping from her man's eye as she dabbed at her own. She smiled at the thought of her tough mountain man being strong enough to let his emotion show, even to the measure of one tear.

WITH SPRING WELL UNDER WAY, the aspen were showing their buds and a few had strutted a few leaves out, the days were getting a little longer and the sun was considerably warmer. Tate pulled up atop a ridge overlooking the valley of Embargo Creek. He scanned the valley with his brass scope and within moments saw some coyotes fighting off ravens and whiskey jacks over the carcass of what appeared to be a horse. He slipped the scope back in his saddlebags and kneed Shady forward, to the bottom of the valley. As he approached, coyotes scattered and birds flew. It was the carcass of a horse, and Tate stepped down to search the area for the remains of the men. They were just a short distance away, in a cluster of rocks that had apparently been their last breastwork.

He hesitated for a moment, then ground tied Shady and walked to the remains. The bones had been pretty well picked clean, but scraps of buckskin and clothing and boots remained, enough so he could identify each of the bodies. While Old Bill had been considerably taller than his companions, it was easy to identify his. Tate returned to his horse, untied the shovel from behind the cantle, and returned to start the graves.

The cluster of rocks were near the tree line and he dug the graves nearby. After covering them with rocks, he carved a single cross on one tree and two crosses on another. He stood between the trees and the graves, and opened his Bible to read from Psalm 91 verse 11 and 14, *For He shall give his angels charge over thee, to keep thee in all thy ways. Because he hath set his love upon me, therefore will I deliver him: I will set him on high, because he hath known my name.*

"Well, Bill, just like you figgered. But, I know you knew the Lord as your Savior so I'm certain you're up there with Him now. So, Lord, you take care of Old Bill. He done a lot for you down here, what with translating the Bible for the Osage Indians, teachin' 'em the Word, and tellin' a whole lot o' folks about Jesus. They don't come much better'n him." Tate dropped his head, pushed a rock back a little closer to the others, picked up the shovel and went back to Shady, who was croppin' grass in the shade of the pines.

"Well, boy. You've had a good roll, a good rest, and some mighty fine new grass. Now, that there sun has already slipped past them mountains and dusk is weighin' heavy on us, but I'm anxious to get back to muh woman. What say we travel by the stars?" Shady lifted his head and looked at Tate, nodded as if he understood every word, and dropped his nose to the grass for another bite.

CHAPTER THIRTY-SIX
FAMILY

HE RACED THE FIRST GREY LIGHT OF MORNING BACK TO THE village hoping to crawl into the blankets before the day started. The moon was still hanging drowsily above the western mountains as he slipped through the entry and crawled to the blankets. But what he found in the blankets shocked him. Instead of the welcoming arms of Morning Sky, it was the snoring form of Two Eagles. When Tate bumped into him, they both jumped to their feet as if being attacked!

"What are you . . . where's my wife?" asked Tate, still in a crouch with a knife in his hand.

The gruff voice of Two Eagles answered, "She is with my woman. They have been busy all night and sent me away. Women!" he spat.

Tate looked to see stirring among the other blankets and realized Sean and the animals were huddled together on top of a buffalo robe. He put his knife away, dropped to the ground and grabbed a blanket and without another word, curled up in his covers. He was disappointed, but tired enough to stretch out and let sleep cover his eyes.

When he awoke, the sun was well up in the sky and the tipi was empty. He stretched and rose, stepped from the lodge to see Morning Sky tending the fire and stirring a pot. She reached for a cup, poured some coffee, and handed it to her man who accepted it with a smile. "So, how's Red Bird?"

Maggie smiled widely, poured herself a cup of java, and sat beside her husband on the blanket. "She's fine, and so's the baby," she declared, pulling her feet to the side and under her.

Tate seated himself cross legged on the blanket and sipped on his coffee. He asked, "So?"

"It's a big healthy boy. Two Eagles is with them now, and he's so proud I don't know if he'll fit through the entry of the tipi to get out. You men are all alike, we women do all the work and you strut around like peacocks!" she giggled.

"I saw a peacock once, back in Missouri. Purty thing, but noisy!"

"Ummmhummm, just like you men."

They bumped shoulders and laughed at each other, happy together in the warm sun. Tate looked around, "Where's the rest of the family?"

Maggie laughed, "Family are they? If you mean our son and his animals, they went down to the creek with some of the other boys. He'll be back soon. It's good for him to be with other kids, and Lobo and Buster take care of him like he's part of their pack."

Tate looked up to see Two Eagles approaching and stood to meet his friend. "Well, I see you're smiling like a proud papa," and reached out his hand for the usual greeting.

"My lodge and my heart are full today. He will be a fine warrior one day."

"I'm sure he will and if he takes after his father, he will also be a good leader of the people."

Maggie offered him a cup of coffee which he declined,

but he seated himself beside his friends. He looked up at Tate and said, "Our scouts tell us a herd of buffalo are moving into the valley. It is the first herd of the season and we will wait until they have moved north of the valley of the big river that you call Rio Grande, and we will move behind them."

"That's wise. If you start a stampede and they turn back south, that could discourage any other herds moving into the valley," replied Tate, thoughtfully.

"We will wait for word from our scouts before we move."

Tate nodded and Maggie interjected, "Red Bird tells me you will not choose a name for your son until he shows you what his name is to be, is that right?"

"Yes, and the honor of naming the child will go to the brother of the father," answered Two Eagles as he looked at Tate.

Tate was surprised at the implication and motioned to himself with a questioning look on his face. The village chief said, "You gave me the honor of naming your son, Little Bear. It is only right that you choose the first name for my son."

"Well, I never expected that, it might take me a while to find the right name."

"Your son was walking before I gave him his name, so . . . " and with a motion of his hand, Two Eagles implied Tate had plenty of time to come up with just the right name for his son.

It was the second day after the birth of the chief's son when the scouts came rushing back into camp, announcing the herd was in position for their hunt. The men of the village had been preparing for the hunt and each had their buffalo pony tethered near their lodge, as did Tate. The women had not been idle, knowing their work required sharp knives, hatchets, and lodgepoles for travois to haul the bounty back to camp. Tate brought both the dapple grey for Maggie and the piebald pack-mare for their travois and tethered them nearby. When the announcement sounded, the village began to hum with activity and Two Eagles rode up to the lodge of Tate and Maggie, motioning for Tate to follow. Tate looked at his redhead, she nodded for him to go ahead, and she started for the lodge of Red Bird.

They had already discussed the hunt and they knew Red Bird would not miss out, but Maggie was determined to relieve her of much of her duties as she could. Maggie was of the mind of white women, that believed that a new mother should be bed-ridden for at least a week, but Red Bird walked in the way of the people and was busy about her duties the same day as the delivery. As she neared the lodge of her friend, Maggie saw Red Bird busy readying the travois on their packhorse in anticipation of a good hunt. Maggie was shaking her head in disbelief as she approached her friend, "Red Bird, let me help you. Where's that new boy at?"

The new mother motioned to the still form, bound tightly in the cradleboard and leaning against the hide lodge, with busy eyes watching all the activity. Maggie stood with hands on her hips and looked from the boy to the woman as Red Bird said, "He is a good baby. He knows his mother has much to do and he watches."

Both women looked up as they heard the horde of hunters ride from the village. They looked at one another, grinned and Maggie said, "I'll wait at my lodge. I still need to load our packs, but I will be ready soon." Red Bird nodded and watched her friend turn and leave.

IT WAS WELL after dark when the feasting began. The successful hunt brought a cheerful spirit to the village and the many cookfires had full pots and skewered meats. A

dance had begun for those that still had the energy to partici-
pate, but most were too tired and more concerned with
eating and turning in for the night. When Tate and Maggie
joined a very full Lobo and Buster, and a very tired Sean in
the lodge, it took little time for the family to soon be quiet
and asleep. They had already decided to start their journey
home in the morning, and they were happy at rest.

Come morning, Maggie walked beside Red Bird, arm in
arm with her friend. The new addition rode happily in the
cradleboard on Red Bird's back and the women shared the
time quietly. Tate had the horses ready, Sean already
mounted behind the cantle of his dad's saddle and Lobo and
Buster stretched out on their bellies, as they all waited for
Maggie. She looked at her family, back at Red Bird, "I'll be
watching for you 'bout the end of summer. I won't have all
the women around me that you did, and I'll be counting
on you."

"We will be there," and looking at Tate, "and maybe you
will have a name for our son."

Tate grinned at the new mother and answered, "I'll be
workin' on it, but we might have to wait til that boy shows us
a thing or two about what his name is supposed to be."

As the small entourage rode from the camp, many came
alongside to say their goodbyes, including several of the
youngsters that had spent time with Sean and his animals. It
was a pleasant time, and as all goodbyes, somewhat sad.
However, the thought of going home put smiles on all their
faces and even Lobo and Buster seemed to be anxious to get
back to the tall timber. Three days would see them across the
valley and into the clearing and home.

CHAPTER THIRTY-SEVEN
FALL

TATE STOOD OVER THE CARCASS OF THE SPIKE BULL ELK HE HAD downed with his longbow. He was north of their cabin and still in the Sangre de Cristo mountains, on the west slope and on a shoulder that gave a wide view of the valley floor below. He looked to his south at a wide grove of aspen where he had discovered the beds of several elk and had jumped them to take this prize at his feet. Their larder was almost full and this meat would probably make their preparations complete. He saw the beginning of color change on the far side of the grove, the yellow tinge heralding the coming of the brilliant fall colors, which told of the soon arrival of winter. It was his favorite time of year, the colors of the high mountains strutting their stuff and painting the mountains with gold, orange and even red. When the first snowfall dusted the peaks, and the skirts of timber showed shades of gold, it seemed that God was just showing off His creation with crowning colors.

The air was clear and crisp, the streams were showing crystals of ice, the bull elk were bugling their challenges and the cow elk were grunting their approvals. The bears were putting on their extra fat and winter coats as they prepared their winter quarters. Big-horn sheep were heard crashing their massive curls as they sought to prove who was the best ram of the mountains. Mule deer had shed the velvet and showed their massive racks, parrying with one another for the rights to the waiting does. Sage grouse were donning their winter feathers while they evaded both coyotes and wolves. It was the time of year that every animal had purpose and focus, and the creation of Almighty God held the attention of each and every creature.

Tate bent to his task of dressing out the elk, stripping the hide and de-boning the carcass. Shady and the piebald stood ground tied and doing their best to consume every available tuft of grass within reach. Lobo sat on his haunches ready to catch every scrap that Tate would toss his way. The man made short work of the butchering and transferred the meat to the panniers hanging on the pack saddle, rolled up the hide and tied it to the pack rig between the panniers, and looked at Lobo, as he worked on the rib bone, determined not to let one scrap of meat go to waste. "Come on boy, you can bring that along, but we gotta get back to the cabin. Maggie don't want us to be gone long, not in her condition, no sir."

WHEN HE BROKE from the trees into the edge of the clearing, he was surprised to see four strange horses in the corral. He reined up and stood in the stirrups to get a closer look at the horses. He recognized the Appaloosa mare of Red Bird and the big sorrel stallion of Two Eagles, but the other two were not familiar. He scanned the clearing as much as possible, from the trail that had taken him into the tall timber. He was at the side and slightly behind the cabin and could not see the front porch and main entrance, but he kneed Shady ahead and walked the horse into the clearing. As he cleared the edge of the cabin, he saw two buckskin clad Indian warriors seated on the rockers and visiting with one another. They turned as they heard the horses approach and Tate recognized Two Eagles, but the other man was a stranger, but he could tell this man was a Comanche.

"Ho! Longbow! It is good you return, and you have brought meat. That is good, I thought you would have us go hungry," chided Two Eagles as he stood and started from the porch. Tate reined up, stepped down, and greeted his friend with clasped forearms as they drew one another near and slapped each other's shoulders. Tate watched as the other man stepped from the porch and saw motion at the door as White Feather came out on the porch.

She smiled broadly at Tate and said, "Ah, my brother has returned! It is good to see you. This is my helper and apprentice, Buffalo Running."

At the introduction, the young man stepped forward to greet Tate. "I am honored," he said as he clasped forearms with Tate, who nodded his head and looked to White Feather.

"It is good to see you, I am pleased you are here and I know Morning Sky must be very pleased as well."

THE WOMEN HAD ARRIVED within an hour of one another and their timing could not have been better. Maggie had started thinking her time had arrived as she began having different pains and movements. In that mysterious unspoken communication that women have and men don't understand, both White Feather and Red Bird had known when they were needed and started their journey even before Morning Sky had supposed her time was near. White Feather, the shaman of the Comanche, had tended many women at this time and she took charge, and that included instructing the men that they would not be allowed in the cabin and they must tend to their own needs, including cooking.

Tate put most of the meat on their racks in their cavern, retaining a sizable haunch for the spit. Maggie had prepared a nice pot of vegetables that was surrendered to the men at the cookfire, and a fine meal was under way as the men sat on the logs and tended their duties. Buffalo Running was a little apprehensive of Lobo and Buster, but slowly began to relax as the men watched Little Bear playing with the two furballs of fun.

The coffee pot was emptied, and Tate bent to pick it up, ready to fetch more water when White Feather stepped out on the porch and motioned for him to come. He dropped the pot, and ran to the porch, fearful there was some problem, but the smile on White Feather's face allayed his fears and his questioning look met with, "She is fine and wants to see you."

He stepped into the cabin and two long strides took him to the door of their room and the foot of the bed. Maggie was propped up on pillows and holding a bundled baby in her arms. She smiled at Tate, "Come see your daughter."

Tate chuckled, "A daughter! That's great!" He stepped to the side of the bed and sat with one hip on the edge, and leaned over to pull back the blanket to see his little girl. Thin red hair adorned the red skinned newborn, and a little hand waved in the air. Her chubby cheeks showed matching dimples and her eyes, open just a slit, showed green. He looked from the babe to the mom and said, "Thank goodness, she looks just like you!"

Maggie giggled, "Aye, I have to agree with you there. She's a fine little lassie. And what are we going to name her?"

"As we discussed, Sadie, after my mother, and Marie, after your mother."

Maggie smiled and nodded as she looked down at the infant and said, "Sadie Marie Saint."

And so it was, that the Rocky Mountains gained another Saint.

A LOOK AT WAPITI WIDOW
(ROCKY MOUNTAIN SAINT 7)
BY B.N. RUNDELL

She had the complexion of weathered leather, eyes like shining lumps of coal, a voice that grated like a rasp, and she was a skilled gunsmith with the demeanor of a wolverine. But she had a set of twins that needed to be raised and the city was no place for that. And when the wagon train she joined was hit by Indians and she and her family were left behind, her skill with a big Sharps rifle made her a welcome addition to a buffalo hunt with the Comanche. But her goal was the gold fields of California and she needed help. Only one man in the mountains could handle that task, Tate Saint, known as the Rocky Mountain Saint, and his family would soon provide all the help she needed, and more besides. But an attack by the same Jicarilla Apache and Mouache Ute that wiped out Fort Pueblo on Christmas day, would put them all to the test, and that wasn't all that would be thrown at them by the forces of nature, the wilds of the wilderness and the depravity of man. Challenges and trials would come against them, and the mettle of the mountain man would have to prove its worth, if he was up to it.

AVAILABLE NOVEMBER 2018 FROM B.N. RUNDELL AND
WOLFPACK PUBLISHING

ABOUT THE AUTHOR

Born and raised in Colorado into a family of ranchers and cowboys, B.N. Rundell is the youngest of seven sons. Juggling bull riding, skiing, and high school, graduation was a launching pad for a hitch in the Army Paratroopers. After the army, he finished his college education in Springfield, MO, and together with his wife and growing family, entered the ministry as a Baptist preacher.

Together, B.N. and Dawn raised four girls that are now married and have made them proud grandparents. With many years as a successful pastor and educator, he retired from the ministry and followed in the footsteps of his entrepreneurial father and started a successful insurance agency, which is now in the hands of his trusted nephew. He has also been a successful audiobook narrator and has recorded many books for several award-winning authors. Now finally realizing his life-long dream, B.N. has turned his efforts to writing a variety of books, from children's picture books and young adult adventure books, to the historical fiction and western genres

https://wolfpackpublishing.com/b-n-rundell/